A Candlelight Ecstasy Romance®

"DON'T LOOK SO TRIUMPHANT," SHE REMARKED CROSSLY.

"Ah, no, Abby." He smiled tenderly. "Just shocked right down to my toes."

"Shocked? Aren't women of my age and position allowed to enjoy an occasional kiss?"

"Oh, yes, indeed." Clint grinned again. "And I intend seeing that it happens on a regular basis. Have dinner with me tonight."

"Sorry, I already have a date."

"Break it," Clint demanded.

"I don't break dates," she said evenly. "Besides, being a widow with limited opportunities, I have to take advantage of each one that comes my way."

"Cal Densen is a boy, Abby, and a boy is not what you need. You're aching for a man to make love to you. Don't mistake the two."

"And you think that you're that man?" she asked derisively.

"I don't think, sweetheart, I *know* I am. And so will you before it's over."

CANDLELIGHT ECSTASY ROMANCES®

WHERE LOVE MAY LEAD

Eleanor Woods

A CANDLELIGHT ECSTASY ROMANCE®

Published by
Dell Publishing Co., Inc.
1 Dag Hammarskjold Plaza
New York, New York 10017

Dell ® TM 681510, Dell Publishing Co., Inc.
Candlelight Ecstasy Romance®, 1,203,540, is a registered
trademark of Dell PublishingCo., Inc., New York, New York.

ISBN: 0-440-19747-3

Printed in the United States of America

First printing—April 1985

To Our Readers:

We have been delighted with your enthusiastic response to Candlelight Ecstasy Romances®, and we thank you for the interest you have shown in this exciting series.

In the upcoming months we will continue to present the distinctive, sensuous love stories you have come to expect only from Ecstasy. We look forward to bringing you many more books from your favorite authors and also the very finest work from new authors of contemporary romantic fiction.

As always, we are striving to present the unique, absorbing love stories that you enjoy most—books that are more than ordinary romance. Your suggestions and comments are always welcome. Please write to us at the address below.

Sincerely,

The Editors
Candlelight Romances
1 Dag Hammarskjold Plaza
New York, New York 10017

CHAPTER ONE

"Damn!" Abby muttered as she felt the tiny earring back slip from her fingers and fall to the floor. The morning was turning into one of those complete fiascoes that made one want to crawl back into bed and pull the covers up over one's head. Already she'd broken a glass, found a button missing from the blouse she'd wanted to wear, and received a telephone call from her father.

At the rate I'm going, she thought disgustedly as she crouched on the floor of the bathroom and began searching for the earring back, *I'll probably wind up as a receptionist at a funny farm.* She'd already learned that going out on job interviews had a way of turning a normally happy person into something of a grouch.

She finally spotted the tiny gold object and was getting to her feet when the phone rang. "Wonderful!" she let explode with such force that Sarge, the lazy black cat who allowed Abby to be his mistress and who was dozing on the foot of her bed, opened his eyes and glared at her.

Abby stalked through to the adjoining bedroom and over to the table beside the bed. She grabbed up the receiver.

"Yes?"

"Good morning, Abby." Laura Temple's voice sounded amused. "You seem to be in a beautiful mood this morning."

"Sorry." Abby grinned in spite of herself. "I thought it might be the Major again. He's already brightened my day for at least thirty minutes this morning. What can I do for you?"

"I think I may have found the perfect job for you," Laura said brightly. Too brightly to suit Abby. She'd learned long ago that when her normally calm friend and neighbor got that quiver of nervousness in her voice and attempted to hide it with exaggerated eagerness, she was usually up to something.

"Exactly where is this job, and what is it?" she asked cautiously.

"It's here in the same building where I work, and it's an opening for an administrative assistant."

"Why didn't you mention it last night at dinner?"

"Because it came up very unexpectedly. And I wanted to check out the details before I called you," Laura explained. "The woman who had the position recently found out she was pregnant. She's been having some trouble, and when she saw her doctor yesterday, he ordered her to stay in bed for several months. Can you be here within the hour?"

"The thought of being an administrative assistant to anyone is terrifying," Abby told her. "Besides, I have an appointment at ten with a Miss Johnson."

"Forget about Miss Johnson," Laura said quickly. "Jobs like this one don't happen along every day, sweetie."

"What about typing and shorthand? Even though I'm taking a refresher course in office skills, I seriously doubt anyone in their right mind will be willing to hire me once they see how rusty I am at the typewriter. As for dictation—"

"Stop thinking up excuses, Abby. Just get yourself down here. And be sure and dress sharp. The gentleman you'll be seeing likes the women who work for him to have good clothes sense."

"Why?" Abby asked mutinously. "Is he some sort of lecherous old man?"

"Not at all." Laura sighed. "He simply runs a tight ship and expects his employees to do their part. Stop being so pessimistic. You want a job: I think I've found one for you."

"But my typing—" Abby spluttered, only to find herself talking to the buzz of the dial tone.

She dropped the receiver, then turned and stared thoughtfully at Sarge and Fred, the small black schipperke who had wandered into the bedroom. "Well, kids, it seems that Auntie Laura has been a busy girl this morning. I have no earthly idea what an administrative assistant does, but it looks as though I'm about to find out."

Abby stepped from the elevator, her feet sinking into a sinfully deep sea of beige carpeting that

11

seemed to stretch endlessly across the large reception area and down a long corridor.

Laura, whose desk faced the elevator and who was talking on the phone, motioned Abby to a chair. She covered the mouthpiece with her hand. "I'll be with you in a sec. I'm glad you wore that color—peach looks super on you."

I wish I felt super, Abby thought to herself as she sat down, *rather than like a lamb being led to slaughter.*

"Now," Laura said briskly a few minutes later as she cradled the receiver, "let's talk about this job. You can start immediately, can't you?"

"I'm not sure," Abby replied, startled. "I mean, what would I be doing? Who would I be working for?" She leaned forward. "Honestly, Laura, I don't really think—"

"Don't you dare start in with all that garbage about not being able to do it, Abby," her friend hissed. "You are a master of diplomacy. You've had to be to get along with the Major. You're also intelligent, pretty, and a quick learner. That's all you need."

"There has to be a catch," Abby said stubbornly at the exact moment the doors of the elevator could be heard swishing open.

"Laura, have you had a chance to get started on a replacement for Rita?"

Abby turned and stared at the tall, dark haired man, with skin so tanned it looked as though he'd spent his entire life outdoors. Heavy black brows were drawn together in an irritated line above a pair of gray eyes as cold and biting as the overcast sky on a brisk winter morn. His nose was hawkish, and there was the suggestion of steel in the unyielding sweep of his jaw and his square, cleft chin.

The jacket of the charcoal suit covered a pair of shoulders that even Abby's untrained eye could see were wide and powerful, not needing the skillful touch of the tailor's needle to produce an attractive silhouette.

"I believe I have the perfect replacement, Clint," Laura replied. "This is Abby Dunbar. Abby, meet Clint Weston, my boss."

With an expression akin to horror plainly showing on her face, Abby forced herself to meet the hard, openly appraising gaze of the man who, in the meantime, had walked over and was casually leaning against the desk, his long arms crossed over his chest. The height and breadth of him reminded her of the sword of Damocles—hanging over her head.

"Mr. Weston," she said quietly, her fingers gripping the soft leather of her purse for dear life. *Damn Laura!* Abby thought furiously. *How dare she introduce me to this—this Genghis Khan she's always complaining about.*

"Miss Dunbar." Clint tipped his head forward the barest fraction of an inch, his steady gaze never leaving her face. "Has Laura explained the different aspects of the position to you?"

Abby took a deep breath before answering. She knew for certain that nothing on earth could induce her to work for this intimidating man. Why, from the moment he'd entered the room, the

13

atmosphere had surged alive, as though some supercharged force were pulsating throughout the entire area and the people within.

"Actually, Mr. Weston," she began, "I was about to tell Laura that I've already made tentative arrangements to take a job somewhere else." She gave Laura, who was staring at her with open dismay, an apologetic smile. "I hope you understand, but I do feel obligated."

"What a pity," said Clint, his gaze sweeping back and forth between the two women as he picked up on the undercurrents of conflict coursing between them. "Laura seems to have an excellent knack for filling the vacancies that occasionally occur in my personal staff. But if you've already made other arrangements, then I suppose that's it."

"Oh, but she hasn't gone that far, I'm sure," Laura said quickly, giving her friend a hard look. "You haven't, have you, Abby?"

"No, but I—" Abby shrugged. "I—"

"Then it certainly won't hurt to talk with Clint for a few minutes," the blonde said smoothly. She gave her boss a pleasant smile. "I really do think Abby would be perfect for the job. You have enough time now to interview her if you'd like."

"Well, then, Miss Dunbar." Clint smiled, and the transformation of his harsh features almost took Abby's breath away. "Unless you're in a hurry, why don't we go into my office and chat?"

Before she could answer, Abby found her elbow clasped in a firm grip and felt herself being brought to her feet. She was ushered past a pleased Laura and down a long, carpeted corridor.

Moments later she and Genghis Khan—*no, no*, she hurriedly chastised herself, *I mustn't think that way, at least not now*—entered an office whose bold decor bore Clint Weston's stamp.

"Why don't you have a seat, Miss Dunbar," he suggested, "while I make one quick telephone call." He seated himself in a massive chair behind the desk, then reached for the telephone. After dialing he swung around so that his back was to Abby.

Not wishing to give the impression that she was listening to his conversation with someone he called Alana, Abby chose instead to let her gaze wander around the spacious office. Each fixture in the room, from the oversized desk to the heavy brass ashtrays scattered throughout, was large and sturdy—in perfect keeping with the man.

This entire situation is incredible, she decided rather dazedly as she deliberately kept her eyes trained on *things* rather than on Clint Weston. *This man is even more overbearing than the Major, and Laura knows it. She also knows I don't care for men who think they own the world.*

Without her being aware of it Abby's face had taken on a mulish expression, her brow puckering in consternation. As soon as Mr. High and Mighty Weston finished his telephone conversation, she'd politely thank him for seeing her, then leave.

Clint swung back around and cradled the receiver, his eyes filling with amusement as he saw

15

the defiant lift of Abby's chin and the less than pleased expression on her face.

"So—Miss Dunbar, am I to understand that you aren't working at the moment?"

"That's correct." Abby nodded. "However, I would like to clear up one small detail before we go any further. It's Mrs. Dunbar. I'm a widow. I'm also quite sure that I wouldn't be able to fit into your organization."

"Why not?" Clint asked bluntly. He couldn't put his finger on it, but there was something about the small, pretty brunette that interested him. All the hiring for his corporation was handled by a well qualified personnel director, with the exception of his personal staff. Over the years he'd learned that, owing to the overlapping of their work, the replacement of his receptionist, his secretary, or his administrative assistant was best handled by allowing the two remaining ones to have some say in choosing the newest member of the team.

This was the first time, though, that Clint had found himself in the position of trying to convince someone to come to work for his firm. It was challenging, and he did like a challenge. There was also Laura's opinion to consider. She'd been with him long enough to know his likes and dislikes. She obviously felt Abby Dunbar had what it took to become a viable part of the operation.

"Why not, Mrs. Dunbar?" he asked again, watching the play of emotions on Abby's face as she struggled to answer. "You look like an intelligent person," he went on. "And I know Laura well enough to be sure that if she thinks you can do the job, you can. I fail to see the problem."

"As I told you earlier, I'm not working at the moment. As a matter of fact, Mr. Weston, I've never worked a single day in my entire life. And quite frankly"—she pursed her lips in a rueful slant—"the thought of working for you is terrifying."

"Really?" Clint smiled, and again Abby found herself amazed by the change that the simple flexing of facial muscles brought to his face. "Well, I hate to disappoint you, but I haven't eaten a single administrative assistant for breakfast in months."

"You're making me sound foolish," Abby replied coolly.

"Not at all." Clint dismissed the charge with a casual flick of one large hand. "I'm merely attempting to point out to you that you've blown the entire matter out of proportion. As for your inexperience, I've found it's far easier to train a beginner than to undo someone else's mistakes." He stared thoughtfully at her for several seconds. "Are you really considering another job?"

Abby fidgeted beneath his bold stare, wishing for some means of escape, some way of quietly but abruptly finding herself back in the security of her nice cozy apartment. "No." She shrugged resignedly. "I'm afraid not. When Laura called me, she left out the pertinent details. Needless to say, when I learned more about the job, I panicked."

"Then why don't you give it a try?" he suggested. "Believe it or not, I can be very patient. Three months should let us know whether or not you will fit into our organization."

"Even though I can't type very well or take shorthand?" she asked in the hope of hearing him say that without those two skills he wouldn't be able to use her.

But he didn't, and as they talked further Abby found herself agreeing to the three-month trial period, then felt her jaw drop at the salary. By the time she left Clint's office and made her way back to Laura, she felt as though she'd been run through the same kind of automatic car wash she took Betsy to every other week.

"I think—no, I'm positive it's the dirtiest trick anyone has ever played on me," she remarked acidly to a grinning Laura as they sat eating lunch a short while later.

"Don't be such a pessimist," Laura said lazily. She leaned back in her chair and regarded the scowling Abby. "Think how relieved your father will be when he hears that you won't be working as a hostess at the Golden Gull."

That remark did bring a smile to Abby's face. "The poor Major. I'm certain he thinks his once sane and dutiful daughter has gone completely off her rocker."

"Well, I think it's about time," Laura firmly reminded her. "For as long as I've known you, you've let him push and pull you about like a rubber ball on a string. I've never known a man to be so obsessed with dominating everyone within his reach."

"I suppose it comes from being in the military for so many years," Abby mused. "He's army from head to toe. I honestly believe it was that rigid exactness in him that caused my mother to leave him. My only regret is that she died before she had a chance to enjoy life."

"When do you plan on telling him about your job?"

"I haven't had time to think about it, thanks to you. When I decided to find the real me, I didn't expect to become employed by your slave driver of a boss. I must confess it's left me rather breathless."

"You'll adapt," Laura said encouragingly. "In no time at all you'll have Clint eating out of your hand."

"Now, I wonder why that very worthy suggestion fails to evoke the slightest bit of warmth within my heart?" she replied curtly, pinning her friend with a frosty glare. "Let him eat out of your hand. He probably bites anyway."

They parted outside the restaurant, with Laura pleased as punch about having landed her friend such a cushy position. As for Abby, she found herself debating whether to show up the next morning or to pack a bag and take a vacation.

By the time she was in her car and headed home, she was convinced the latter was the best solution. She'd heard Laura complain on more than one occasion about how difficult Clint Weston could be. *So why did you accept the job?* she asked herself and immediately hated the answer. Once again she'd allowed someone stronger to make a decision that she should have made herself. And yet common sense told her that her lack of training narrowed her career choices considerably.

She'd been groomed and educated since birth to attain one ultimate goal in life—to be a "good" military wife. She thought back on her brief marriage to Corey, and her father's disappointment that his son-in-law hadn't been connected with some branch of the military.

But Corey, like her, had been involved in his own private war—trying to live his own life in spite of an older domineering brother. *God!* Abby slowly shook her head. *What a pitiful pair we were. Two misfits with little or no courage, each seeking strength and comfort from a kindred soul.*

Never again, she vowed as she made the turn into the parking lot of her apartment building, *will I allow another person to dominate my life as my father has done.*

CHAPTER TWO

Abby paused after entering her apartment and let the quiet peacefulness of the room flow over her. Thank God it was Friday!

It had been three weeks now since that morning when Laura had called and said she'd found Abby a job. Three weeks of trying to master a routine that, at first, had seemed as complicated as the security system at Fort Knox.

She tossed her purse onto a chair, kicked off her shoes, and headed for the sofa, where she collapsed.

Clint Weston was an absolute demon to work for. And each day she was there, he seemed to require more of her.

She thought, rather grimly, of the salary that had at first appeared to be so generous. *Considering my hectic schedule, I'll probably be old and gray before I'm able to spend a penny of it.*

In all her life she'd never known a man with such drive. *Indefatigably* was hardly an adequate word to describe the way he oversaw and controlled the varied operations of his corporation. To a newcomer such as Abby it appeared that Weston, Inc. had a finger in everything from oil to ranching—maybe even potholders and Band-Aids.

"No wonder his wife divorced him," she muttered as she thrust an arm behind her head and stared at the ceiling. "I'm sure she had to make an appointment to see him—and was, more likely than not, told to wait." For a moment she wondered what the two former Mrs. Westons had been like. She'd learned, through Laura, of course, that his first wife had died shortly after they were married. His second marriage had ended in divorce.

With an angry toss of her head she returned to her own personal torture at the hands of her esteemed boss during these last three weeks. James Gardner, Clint's secretary, and Laura had proved invaluable in helping her overcome her initial fear of taking on the awesome responsibility of her job.

"Genghis isn't such a bad person to work for, you know," James told her on one occasion when Abby was fighting her way through an avalanche of appointments, files, and complaints from two department heads.

A dull flush spread over her features as she met the dancing devils of amusement in the secretary's eyes. "I can see now that my friend Laura has a big mouth."

"Don't let it bother you." James chuckled. "Our fearless leader has been called worse."

"I can well imagine," Abby agreed. "His temper should be classified as one of the ten most dangerous weapons against mankind."

James laughed. "I see you've already felt the sharp edge of his tongue. What was your reaction?"

"For a moment I was tempted to retaliate in kind." She grinned, then shrugged. "But considering the job market and the fact that he'd been forced to deal with several annoying individuals that particular morning, I refrained from getting myself sacked."

"Next time don't be so understanding. He'd a lot rather you answer him right back than suffer in silence. But don't worry, you'll soon learn how to handle him. Just as you're learning this job."

She looked skeptically at James. "The boss? I'll never learn how to handle him. But the job is another story."

And I will learn, she told herself as she flexed the muscles of her back and shoulders, then stretched. *I'll never be the quiet dormouse again, ready to do my father's bidding without regard for my own wants and needs. I've always heard there's nothing worse than a person who's kicked some addiction. I wonder what happens when a heretofore passive woman decides to take command of her life?*

"I might have the Major pretty well under control, but I still have to master Mr. Weston." Abby closed her eyes and shuddered. Being in control of one's destiny was one thing. Standing up to that gray-eyed maniac was quite another.

Her brow furrowed as she thought back to one of several unpleasant encounters with her employer that made her want to box her own ears for her lack of courage.

It was her second week on the job. James was having to spend endless hours putting together a bid on a refinery Weston was interested in constructing, leaving Abby on her own to deal with the boss.

Clint came roaring into her office shortly after she'd arrived at her desk and told her to be ready in an hour to go with him to a certain job site. Abby merely blinked and nodded, her tongue glued to the roof of her mouth.

"Take along your cassette recorder and the camera," he reeled off, not bothering to look up from the report he was scanning.

Even at that early hour, Abby noted, the sleeves of his white shirt were rolled up, revealing tanned forearms liberally covered with dark hair. The top buttons of his shirt were undone, and his tie was loosened. And though his presence more often than not filled her with a sense of trepidation, Abby found herself becoming more and more intrigued with this frustrating man. Not that she was attracted to him, she kept telling herself—never. It was simply his vitality, his command over everything and everyone around him.

Apparently satisfied that all was in order, Clint slapped the sheaf of papers down on Abby's desk with such force that she jumped. This brought an amused chuckle from him and caused a profusion of pink to color Abby's cheeks. "Don't look so frightened," he said huskily as he suddenly placed his palms against the surface of her desk and leaned uncomfortably close. "I like my women to be a great deal more sophisticated—and a lot more fiery."

Abby's blue eyes widened with embarrassment as she stared at the fullness of his lips, at the tiny crisscross of lines visible at the corners of his bedeviling gray eyes. The heavy growth of his sideburns clung close and crisp against the sides of his face, and for one infinitesimal moment she felt the most peculiar urge to reach out and run her fingertips over that raven roughness.

"Have you always been such a meek, submissive little thing, Abby?" Clint rasped in the stillness that hung over them. "Was that the type of woman your husband demanded?"

At the mention of Corey's name Abby somehow found the strength to break the incredible spell his presence had cast over her. She pushed back her chair and began rearranging an already neat stack of files.

"My life with my husband is personal, Mr. Weston, and I'd like to keep it that way," she answered quietly, praying he wouldn't hear the awful pounding of her heart.

"It's been sixteen months now since your husband died. That's a long time to keep yourself hidden from the world, Abby," he said softly, his gaze sweeping over the inviting pinkness of her lips and the rounded outline of her small, firm breasts.

"I'm not hiding from anything," she replied with amazing calm, considering the fact that she was being inspected like a side of beef. "I do—or did—quite a bit of volunteer work. It's very rewarding helping those less fortunate than others." The entire time she was talking Abby kept her eyes lowered. She couldn't explain it, but there was something about Clint Weston that frightened her. This wasn't the first time he'd made some remark regarding her private life, but it was the first time he'd gone beyond that invisible line of courtesy.

"Was there something else?" she finally managed to say, willing herself to look up and meet the faintly mocking gleam in his eyes.

"Nothing else, Mrs. Dunbar." His smile was thin. He straightened up. "Aren't you relieved?" Before Abby could reply, he was striding toward the door of his private office. Just before he disappeared, though, he turned. "Talk to James or Laura. Either of them can tell you what to expect on our outing."

Abby's reflective mood was suddenly shattered as all fifteen pounds of Sarge landed on her chest, his motor running full blast. "They've been wonderful helping me learn to cope with everything except my boss," she said quietly.

She reached up and began scratching the cat behind his ears, grinning at his ridiculous slant-eyed, droopy-whiskered face. "Men are strange creatures, Sarge," she murmured. "Do you keep your women in constant anxiety, or are you the strong, silent type?"

Sarge considered the question unworthy of an answer. He gave a decisive flick of his long tail and raised the volume of his raucous engine by several decibels. After a few more minutes of ear scratching Abby unceremoniously dumped her feline friend on the floor and got to her feet. Laura would be arriving any minute now, demanding her cup of coffee.

As she walked past the built-in bookcase on her way to the kitchen, her gaze fell on the picture of Corey taken during one of their weekends in Galveston. She paused and stared thoughtfully at the smiling face of the man who, more than anyone else, was responsible for her becoming a person rather than remaining a timid, frightened creature.

She relived the moment of his death, still saddened that someone as kind and gentle as Corey could be taken so quickly. One moment they were laughing over some crazy, funny story he'd told as they fixed dinner—and the next he was clutching his chest and slipping to the floor.

Naturally the Major and Leon, Corey's brother, took over. "A woman is incapable of handling such matters," she remembered them telling her. And being the dutiful daughter she'd always been, Abby did as she was told. When she wanted to have Corey's body cremated as had been his wish, Leon objected.

"How uncaring, Abby," he tut-tutted in that prim and proper manner she hated. "I'm sure Corey wasn't serious when he mentioned such a thing. We'll have a private funeral, with burial in the family crypt."

Again Abby relented. Even when she finally

27

found the courage to sell the house where she'd lived for most of her married life, she felt guilty for going against Leon's wishes. Naturally he washed his hands of her, a fact she was heartily grateful for later. Leaving that house was a tremendous step for Abby. In some ways, however, she was like a child taking its first halting steps toward maturity.

After her initial decision not to allow, or rather not to invite people to walk on her, at the beginning of her quest for independence, she was forced to take a long, hard look at herself. What she saw wasn't pleasant.

Without meaning to or even being aware that it had happened, she had become a faceless person, a walking, smiling "thing" that was afraid of her own shadow. Afraid to go against whoever happened to be in command of her life at the moment.

With a disgusted toss of her dark head at her own cowardice, she hurried into the kitchen. She added water and grounds to the coffee maker, switched it on, then got out two mugs.

By the time Laura breezed in, Abby had changed into a pair of shorts and a T-shirt and was sitting at the table sipping her coffee.

"Ahh," the tall blonde sighed as she sat down after petting Fred and returning Sarge's narrow-eyed glare. "This just hits the spot. How was your day?"

"Hectic." Abby waved one hand dismissively. "And to think I actually took this job of my own free will." She looked at Laura across the rim of her mug. "Perhaps there's something to be said after all for the meek, unassuming females of this world."

"What?" her neighbor asked bluntly.

"They have peace and quiet for one thing. And they don't feel the need to stand up to impossible bosses."

"Speaking of Clint"—Laura smiled slyly— "how are the two of you really getting along? Each time I've asked that question, I've gotten the stock answer: fine. But underneath that calm facade that comes so naturally to you, how do you really feel about him?"

"If you're thinking of playing cupid, then don't," Abby told her firmly. "Clint Weston makes the Major look like Santa Claus. Besides, he likes his women full of fire—or so he told me."

"Oh? And just how did the subject come up?" Laura asked, her eyes sparkling with inquisitiveness.

"It was during one of the little lectures he's begun favoring me with. The subject of that particular one was my prolonged period of mourning for my husband."

"Your what?" Laura asked in disbelief.

"You heard me," Abby remarked dryly, then continued, "I'm too quiet, too submissive. Yesterday I was informed that a boyfriend would do wonders for my disposition. I believe he said, 'It would add color to your life.'"

"Clint said those things to you?"

"Why the shocked tone?" Abby asked. "I'd

think after working for him as long as you have, you'd be used to the cute little things he says."

"Unfortunately," Laura said with a sigh, "I've never been singled out for his attentions. In fact, I've never known him to take such a personal interest in one of his employees before."

"Well, believe me, I could certainly do without his particular brand of attention."

"Perhaps he's attracted by that unearthly calmness that surrounds you. Why not tell him to butt out when he starts becoming obnoxious?"

"Because I'm determined to keep my job longer than a month," Abby told her. "I hardly think telling my boss to take a hike will keep me employed."

"Nonsense," Laura scoffed. "With most employers you'd probably be correct. But if there's one thing I've learned about Clint, it's that he loves a fight. It goes along with that complex personality of his, I suppose. I've got a pretty good idea he's goading you, hoping to get some reaction from you. Perhaps he wants to learn more about you."

"That's ridiculous. Why should he care what I'm like, as long as I do my job?"

"Because that's the kind of man he is, sweetie. He has a mind like a computer. I've no doubt that what makes each of us tick is stored in his memory like information on a floppy disk."

"My private life is my own affair," Abby maintained stubbornly. "I'm having a devil of a time keeping the Major out of my life. I have no intention of allowing Clint Weston to 'whip' me into shape."

"Oh, well." Laura chuckled. "Forget about him for now. By the way, you haven't changed your mind about this evening, have you?"

"No—but I'll probably regret it. Blind dates can be the pits."

"Not Cal," Laura promised. "He's single, rich, and good-looking."

"Then why on earth are you having to scare up a date for him?" Abby asked. Since being widowed, she'd been approached by more than her share of friends with unattached brothers, cousins, and so on. She'd begun to think there was a special group of men whose sole purpose on earth was to be blind dates for widows, divorcees, and single women in general. She even imagined their motto: Dates for all ages—like Cards for all occasions.

"He and Kip have been working on a case here in Houston most of the week. They still have a lot of research to do, so Kip thought you might like to go to dinner with us. If you and Cal hit it off, we can take it from there."

Cal Densen turned out to be exactly the diversion Abby needed to take her mind off the last three hectic weeks of her life. He was interesting, charming, and just as handsome as Laura had promised.

Dinner was spent with Cal and Kip keeping both women entertained with hilarious anecdotes about some of the cases they'd handled as well as a few youthful scraps they'd gotten into while in law school.

After dinner the foursome made their way to an at the moment "in" club, with an exorbitant cover charge, a minuscule dance floor, tables not much larger than a TV tray, and such subdued lighting as to make one wish for a Seeing Eye dog.

"Isn't this great?" Laura yelled into Abby's ear as they bumped knees trying to sit down.

"No," Abby shouted right back. The old Abby would have politely smiled and agreed, even though she hated it. However, the new Abby was learning that it felt terrific to express an honest opinion.

Unless they wanted to yell at each other, conversation was possible only when the band was taking a break. That left dancing, which Abby enjoyed and at which Cal was excellent. After several fast numbers Abby was convinced her legs would never be the same again. She pleaded exhaustion and breathed a sigh of gratitude when Laura suggested a trip to the powder room.

"Wow!" Abby exclaimed as she collapsed on a brocade-covered stool. "My mind admires his enthusiasm, but my body is protesting like mad. Your friend Cal is unbelievable."

"He's good for you," Laura replied breezily, her hands busy smoothing her hair. "Most of the time you take life too seriously. And even though you go out often enough, most of the men you know are rather—somber."

"I wouldn't call Julian Larson somber," Abby said thoughtfully as she mentally reviewed her list of regulars, as Laura had dubbed them. "Skydiving isn't exactly tame, you know. And"— her eyes danced—"I just might give it a whirl myself."

"You wouldn't!" her friend swiveled around and stared, aghast. "I've never heard of anything so outrageous in my entire life."

"You sound remarkably like the Major. What's so outrageous about skydiving? Every safety precaution is taken."

"You really are considering this harebrained idea?" Laura slowly shook her head.

"Why not?" Abby asked. "You've had most of your life to find yourself, Laura. By trial and error you've rejected what you don't want and chosen what you do. I'm still searching. Not only for a career, any career, but for a sense of personal worth."

Laura was quiet as she considered Abby's remarks. "I suppose I've never thought of it quite like that. You know I'm behind you one hundred percent, kiddo. But do you have to start out by climbing Mount Everest?"

"Perhaps not." Abby laughed. "But I'm excited, Laura. I've come to the conclusion that my marriage to Corey was a period of preparation."

"I'm afraid I don't quite follow you there." Laura frowned as she thought of the man Abby had been married to, with his seemingly unflappable nature. He'd always appeared to be totally dominated by his older brother, Leon.

"In his gentle way he became my buffer. He protected me from my father, and at the same time I was able to see, in him, another person allowing a stronger, more dominating individual —Leon—to take over and control his life. Admittedly Corey was weak. But as I watched him being bent to his brother's will, I began to taste my discontent with my own life."

"Did you and Corey ever talk about this? I mean, was he really aware that Leon dominated him?" Laura asked thoughtfully.

"Oh, yes." Abby sighed. "And he was always finding ways to annoy his brother. At first that shocked me, being indoctrinated as I was to believe that only the strong—always men, of course —were capable of making important decisions— that only they had the *right* to make decisions. But I came to see that that wasn't true. And I suppose in some small way I gave Corey the courage to rebel, just as he gave me the will to fight. I'm sure that wherever he is, he's pulling for me with all his heart and having one hell of a laugh at the Major's reaction to the new me, and the fact that Leon hasn't spoken to me in months."

"So am I," Laura told her. "But all this doesn't change the fact that skydiving is dangerous."

"Maybe." Abby shrugged. "But, then, consider where I'm employed. A month ago nothing on earth could have convinced me that I'd one day be working for Clint Weston. After listening to you gripe and complain about him for years, I'd come to look upon him as some sort of monster."

"And now?"

"He's still a monster, and every morning I look closely at his head for horns and carefully watch

34

his attractive rear when he walks away for some sign of a long tail. The pitchfork is fairly visible because I've felt the sharp points of its prongs a number of times. Believe me, jumping out of a plane will be a piece of cake compared to working for our boss."

Laura sat back, and there was a curious mixture of emotions expressed in the smile that stole over her face. "You know, Abby, we've been friends for a long time. I suppose we know the worst and the best about each other. I've often envied that inner strength, that calmness that has carried you through such a strange and difficult life. Now I find myself envying this determination that's finally emerged in you and the wild and crazy sense of daring I'm seeing. To put it in a nutshell, sweetie, I think you're completely bonkers, but I'm all for you."

"Great." Abby grinned. "It'll be nice having you join me."

"Not on your life!" Laura exclaimed, her eyes round as saucers.

"We'll see." Abby smiled. "We'll see."

They were making their way back across the dark, crowded room toward their table when Abby felt a large hand grasp her wrist and heard an unmistakably familiar voice say, "Well, well, this is a surprise. So you finally decided to take my advice, did you?"

Abby peered needlessly through the smoke-filled dimness, confident she could have identified Clint Weston's voice among hundreds of others through a concrete wall! She also found to her dismay that his wretched face was only inches from her own. So close, in fact, that she caught the distinct aroma of scotch on his breath, which fanned her cheeks.

"Gee, I'm not sure," Abby said, feigning ignorance, uncomfortably aware of Laura standing like a brick wall beside her and listening with avid curiosity to each and every word that was said. "You've given me so many helpful little hints on running my life, I can't seem to get them straight in my mind."

"Well, then, it looks as though I'll have to be more specific in doling out my instructions in the future, won't I?" Abby mumbled an unintelligible reply and sought to remove her wrist from the human handcuff. But that simple gesture on her part merely provoked a tightening of the grip on her wrist. "Hello, Laura," Clint said pleasantly, not in the least embarrassed that his receptionist of several years was grinning outrageously at his antics.

"Clint," Laura responded with a brief nod of her sleek head. "What brings you out to this particular place this evening? I'd have thought that after a long, hard day at the office you would prefer the peace and quiet of a more sophisticated setting."

"I would have," he said flatly. "But the young lady I'm with is from Dallas. Some friends of hers told her about this place and its 'unique' atmosphere. So of course"—and Abby caught the flash of white teeth as he grinned—"I, being the perfect gentleman I am, didn't want to disappoint her."

"I'm sure she'll be properly appreciative," Laura said with open amusement. "Where is she?"

"Dancing. And, yes, I'm certain she will be properly appreciative," Clint replied smoothly. "Otherwise I wouldn't be here. Are the two of you alone?" The question was put to Laura, but it was on Abby that his disturbing gaze lingered.

"No, we're not," Laura said. "And if we don't get back soon, I'm afraid our dates will think we've been kidnapped."

"In that case I won't detain you. If our little mouse here has finally gotten up enough nerve to go out with a real, live man, then I certainly wouldn't do anything to mar her evening." He dropped Abby's wrist and leaned back in his chair. "Perhaps I'll see you before we leave."

Not if I see you first! Abby silently promised herself through clenched teeth as she turned and almost flattened a cocktail waitress in her haste to put some distance between herself and Clint.

"He really does get to you, doesn't he?" Laura chuckled.

"That's putting it mildly."

"I'm almost positive my original idea was correct."

"Which was?"

"I think he's int—er—curious about you. Until you learn to give him as good as you get, I'm afraid you're in for a long siege."

"Then I suppose I'd better start thinking about

looking for another job. I've had about all of his obnoxious prying and cute remarks I can tolerate. I've discovered in the last few weeks that I have a temper."

CHAPTER THREE

Abby tried not to let Clint Weston's presence affect her. But his casual promise that he would see them later filled her with dread. Being forced to deal with him on a day-to-day basis was one thing. Having to endure his insufferable presence in a social situation was something else.

Thus the moment she and Laura returned to their table, Abby was more than happy to oblige Cal and become lost in the crowd of dancers. Perhaps the old adage of Out of sight, out of mind would hold true regarding her boss. She was perfectly willing to let Laura be the one to reap whatever might be the benefits—if any—pandering to Clint's ego.

"I really can't imagine why Laura and Kip haven't introduced us sooner." Cal spoke close to Abby's ear. "Are you seriously involved with someone at the moment and having some fun while he's away?"

Abby chuckled. She met his openly curious grin without resentment. "There's no one particular man in my life, and I prefer it that way. As for our not meeting before now, Laura knows my feelings when it comes to blind dates."

"Ahh." Cal smiled unabashedly. "But aren't you glad you relented and came this evening? Just think of what you'd have missed. I'm single, sort of eligible, and loaded with charm. I've also been told on occasions that I'm handsome. Even in these inflationary times, my dear, I'm somewhat of a bargain as a date."

"Oh, indeed." Abby grinned cheekily. "But what exactly do you mean by 'sort of eligible'?" she asked.

Cal tilted his forehead forward till it rested against Abby's. "I'm sort of eligible until I see wedding bells in a gal's eyes, and then I hightail it to safer ground."

"My, my," she mused solemnly. "And I'd already envisioned us married, with two or three little ones to round out the picture."

"I bet." Cal laughed. "You forget that Laura was quick to let me know that you're no more anxious to stroll down that path than I am."

"True." Abby chuckled. "But I couldn't resist teasing you. Are you always so eager to let it be known that you're a complete coward?"

"Not usually. But meeting a kindred soul gave me courage." He drew her closer. "Will you have dinner with me tomorrow evening?"

"Two dates in a row with the same woman?" she asked in mock surprise. "Aren't you worried that someone will think you're slipping?"

"Definitely not," Cal said with a straight face. "I can risk being seen with you two—even three times. After that I'll have to scout new ground."

"Then by all means let's get the most out of our

allotted time together," Abby replied just as seriously, meeting his dancing eyes with her own laughing ones. "Being seen with you could enhance my reputation beyond words." The conversation was ridiculous and amusing, and exactly what she needed.

"At last," Cal said with a sigh. "I've finally met a woman who appreciates me."

Before Abby could answer in kind, the music ended. A slower-paced number began almost immediately, and a tall dark man materialized beside them.

"I believe you promised me this dance, Abby," Clint said deliberately. Before she had time to do more than blink an eye—or so it seemed—she saw Cal give a light shrug of his shoulders, then turn and walk away. At the same time two strong arms slid around her waist, and Abby found herself being brought close against a hard body that she'd heretofore not only avoided looking at as much as possible but had gone to great lengths to ensure she had no physical contact with.

"Are you always as stiff as a board when you're dancing?" Clint's deep voice broke into the quiet, panic-filled thoughts racing through Abby's mind.

She directed her gaze to the second button of his white shirt and prayed for some sort of release from the paralysis that had caused her tongue to become a stick in her mouth. Allowing this overgrown nerd to intimidate her didn't fit into her concept of the new Abby. They weren't in the office now, and she darn well wasn't going to suffer in silence.

"I can be light as a feather on my feet, Mr. Weston, when I'm dancing with someone I enjoy being with." As soon as the words were out of her mouth, Abby had no trouble at all seeing herself making all over again the long rounds of the various employment agencies.

"Ahh," Clint murmured in an amused voice. "The little mouse has turned into a kitten with claws. How interesting. Is the young man you're with responsible for this sudden change?"

"I doubt it," Abby answered shortly as she tried unsuccessfully to move back from the firm thighs in intimate contact with her own. "Unlike you, he doesn't continuously find ways to insult me."

"Give him time," Clint remarked dryly. "When he finds the ghost of your dead husband hovering between the two of you, he might turn nasty."

This remark did bring Abby's startled blue gaze up to meet the frowning one of her employer. This wasn't the first time he'd implied that she was playing the role of the grief-stricken widow to a degree that bordered on the ridiculous. Aside from the fact that his implications were totally erroneous, it angered her that he considered himself in a position to take her to task.

"How long has it been since anyone told you to mind your own business?" Abby asked bluntly. "If I choose to daily swathe my body in black and let loose with a bloodcurdling wail at ten, two, and four, I can't see how it possibly concerns you." There was anger in her eyes as she spoke—anger and a resigned sense of having burned her bridges behind her.

"I don't believe it." Clint's mouth quirked at the corners. "I've been with you almost every day for three weeks, and you've never shown even the tiniest bit of anger. Now here you are, ready to scratch my eyes out." And to Abby's chagrin he let one long arm slip upward and drew her body, from her neck to her knees, against the solid warmth of him. "Anger becomes you, Mrs. Dunbar. I'll have to remember that in the future."

"Forget the future," Abby muttered ominously. At that moment a soft nudge of his arm caused her nose to be buried in the same spot she'd chosen to stare at only moments ago.

"If I were you, I'd stop struggling," Clint said softly. "People are beginning to stare. To the casual observer it looks as though you're trying to fondle me right here in the middle of the dance floor."

Abby jerked back as far as the bonds of his arms would allow her to, her embarrassed gaze catching the amused grins of a couple directly beside them. She quickly turned her head and stared straight ahead again, wishing the floor would open up and swallow her.

"Would you please let go of me?" she asked in a quietly controlled voice.

"No," Clint said without the slightest hesitation. "Finding that you are capable of showing normal emotions has restored my faith in human nature. Very few people achieve their personal aspirations regarding sainthood, Abby. I haven't yet figured out why you choose to go through life like a shrinking violet, but I will."

Again Abby was forced to raise her eyes and meet the thoughtfully probing gaze of this grim-eyed monster. To her knowledge she'd never been examined by a man as though she were in a laboratory, under a microscope. "You will only learn what I am willing to tell you, Mr. Weston, and as unacceptable as it may seem to you, I haven't the slightest intentions of confiding in you."

Now that she had started, Abby found her tongue tied in the middle and loose at both ends. "I am not some sort of specimen or some weird freak to be taken out when it suits you and probed and examined to your satisfaction. All I'd like from you is a chance to do my job. Prying into my personal life, saintly or not, is not part of the deal."

"Do you know that when you're angry, your eyes change color? Even in this poor excuse for atmosphere I can see the difference. Right now they're dark and stormy, like the sea at war with the elements."

Hadn't he heard her? Abby wondered miserably as she broke the spell of his forceful gaze and looked away. By her standards she'd just insulted him.

Darn him! He could at least give the appearance of being displeased. After all, she thought querulously, it was the first time she had ever done such a thing. But, no, the almighty Clint Weston, confident as a strutting peacock, chose to display his male superiority by patting her on the head, so to speak, and calmly ignoring her outburst.

Abby was frantically searching her mind for something to wound him with, for some sharp barb that would pierce his thick hide, when the music came to an end. But instead of releasing her Clint kept her in the tight circle of his arms, oblivious to the interested looks being directed their way.

"How long were you married, Abby?" he further surprised her by asking.

"A little over two years," she answered without thinking. Now what? Did he have some personal rule or thought concerning that particular subject as well? "Why do you ask?"

"Because you seem remarkably untouched. There's a certain quality of innocence about you that doesn't fit." They continued staring at each other. For Abby it was a moment not unlike others she'd known since meeting Clint. And rather than her finding a barb with which to pierce him, it appeared that he had, as usual, come up with yet another detail about her life, another tidbit with which to goad her.

But Clint wasn't thinking in those exact terms. Abby Dunbar had remained something of a mystery during their three weeks together. He wasn't such an egotist that the slightest rebuff from a woman had him gnashing his teeth. And yet he was curious, he thought as he stared at her.

There was something about her that made him want to protect her, an emotion he hadn't felt in a number of years.

"If you've finished, would you mind releasing me?" Abby asked, breaking the tense silence that had settled over them, blocking out the noise of the crowd milling about them. "I don't usually arrive with one man, then spend a good portion of the evening with another."

"And doing the proper thing is important to you, isn't it, Abby?" Clint asked as he let his hands slide down her arms and hands. He liked the feel of her. She felt smooth and firm, causing him to wonder what it would be like to run his hands over her entire body. He was knowledgeable enough about women to know that, though her breasts were small, they would be well formed, would fit perfectly into the palm of his hand.

"I'm not sure *proper* is the correct word, Mr. Weston," Abby said quietly. "It's more a matter of satisfying myself that I haven't treated anyone unkindly."

"Then by all means hurry over to your young man and 'satisfy' yourself that he hasn't suffered some personal blow to his ego because you left him on his own for a few minutes." He reached out unexpectedly and caressed the side of her cheek with one square-tipped finger, a puzzling smile on his lips. "Though in the future I may remind you of that particular remark."

Abby turned, every nerve ending within her body aware of the tall, dark man beside her, his

46

hand cupping her elbow as he escorted her back to her table.

Instead of leaving, Clint looked expectantly from Laura to the two men, who had risen to their feet. Introductions were made, and though Abby was certain she was imagining it, it appeared to her that her boss was showing a more than casual interest in Cal Densen.

After several minutes of conversation with the members of her party, Clint excused himself. He didn't single Abby out for any sort of specific good-bye, but his entire time at their table had been spent with him standing behind her, his large hands resting on her shoulders. When he left, she felt as though a sudden gust of cold wind had replaced the warmth created by his touch.

Later, after she was home and in bed, she found herself reliving that part of the evening when Clint had entered the picture. She knew she'd overreacted to his taunts, and it annoyed her. She hadn't meant to allow him the pleasure of knowing he could goad her into making a fool of herself, but, she thought with a sigh, that was exactly what she'd done.

It occurred to her that he possessed a special knack when it came to irritating her. She wondered why that was. He wasn't any different from the other men she knew, she kept telling herself. But the truth, even in one's thoughts, wasn't something that could be ignored. Clint was different, and that difference had struck her the moment she first saw him.

Perhaps I resent him because he's begun forc-

ing me to see things about myself I'd rather not dwell on, such as always gravitating toward men who pose no threat to me emotionally; my wretched habit lately of flying off the handle at the slightest inkling that I'm being patronized or that I might be becoming involved in an intimate relationship with a man. I'm not so cold or bitter, she thought caustically, that I want a life without sex or romance. But damn it all—she scowled furiously in the darkness—*I would certainly like to find it on my own, and not with my "beloved" boss breathing down my neck.*

Even when she made an attempt, as she'd tried to do with Clint, to take a stand that would draw attention to her fledgling quest for independence, she knew moments of utter frustration.

Clint had reacted with typical male indulgence, viewing her outburst as a purely feminine ploy, but Abby knew better. She hadn't engaged in an exchange of coy remarks with Clint in order to encourage his interest in her. She wanted the personal satisfaction of knowing she could stand on her own two feet in any given situation, the sense of completeness that a woman has when others accept her as an equal and not simply as a mindless marionette whose strings are being manipulated by someone stronger.

Abby turned over on her side and bunched one end of the pillow beneath her cheek. She was intelligent enough to know that she needed—no, wanted—some romance in her life. The time she'd spent with Corey had left her with a void in her world. She missed the closeness, the quiet moments they'd often spent talking. The more intimate side of their relationship, while not the most exciting, had been adequate. Common sense told her that eventually she would become involved in a relationship with another man. But she also knew it would be with someone who was gentle, someone who was compassionate and caring.

The weekend passed quite pleasantly for Abby. Her date with Cal Densen on Saturday evening was enjoyable, and she agreed to see him again the following night. The only uncomfortable moment during the evening was when Cal asked her if she was also dating Clint Weston.

"Heavens no." She laughed. "I only met the man three weeks ago when I started working for him. Why do you ask?"

Cal cocked his head, his lips thoughtfully pursed as he sought to explain. "I got the distinct impression that he was letting me know, all very subtly of course, that he had a personal interest in you. I'd never met him until last night, but he has a reputation for being tough as granite in his business dealings. I couldn't help but wonder if he employed the same methods in his personal life."

"And I think you've had too much to drink." Abby shook her head dismissively. "My darling boss grates on my nerves, and I on his—like a sore tooth. Other than my job, for which he's training me, we have very little in common. No"—she shrugged her shoulders—"I'm afraid you read more into his asking me to dance than there really is."

"Perhaps," Cal said quietly. "But I'll be curious to see what you have to say on the subject six months from now."

Abby dismissed the idea from her mind until later in the evening when she was back at her apartment and getting ready for bed. The thought of Clint's being interested in her except as someone he could bully was out of the question. He'd already told her, on more than one occasion, what he liked in a woman. He'd even encouraged her to date other men. Did that sound like a man waiting with bated breath to take her out?

But as she was falling asleep Abby couldn't help but remember the way he had caught hold of her wrist when she and Laura first ran into him at his table at the club or the rather proprietary manner in which he'd come onto the dance floor and taken her from Cal. *Good Lord!* she thought fleetingly. *The mere idea of becoming involved with Clint Weston is enough to cause me to seriously consider the blissful escape of a nervous breakdown!*

Monday morning found Abby seated at her desk and up to her elbows in work when she heard Clint approaching. *It's amazing,* she thought as she paused for a moment in her perusal of a file and waited for him to enter. *The floors are thickly carpeted, the walls are insulated, and I can still hear him a good ten seconds before he enters my office. I wonder if anyone has*

*ever introduced Mr. Weston to the gentle art of
entering a room rather than attacking it?*

"Good morning, Abby," the object of her
thoughts said in greeting as he brushed through
the doorway and straight over to perch on the
corner of her desk. "Have you recovered from
your weekend with young Densen?"

Although she wanted to ram the file down his
detestable throat, Abby was forced to admit privately that he brought a certain electric vitality
into the room. Before his arrival the silence had
been overpowering. Now the room fairly crack-
led with expectancy. His personal appearance
wasn't bad either, she grudgingly admitted. He
was dressed in one of the numerous dark suits he
wore, a white shirt opened three buttons down
from the collar and a neat, conservative tie
draped round his neck.

Abby eyed the casualness of his attire and in-
wardly winced. It meant he would change into
work clothes later and charge off to one of the
construction sites with his trusted administrative
assistant at his heels. Perhaps her luck would im-
prove, and he would sprain his ankle within the
next ten minutes.

"If you mean did I enjoy myself, then the answer is yes. Cal is fun to be with," she primly
replied, and hated herself for sounding so pious.
Why couldn't she have come back with a sharp
put-down or a resounding "It's none of your business."

Clint's gray eyes took their own sweet time in
moving over her hair and face and every inch of

her body that was visible above the desk. For a second, Abby was tempted to swing around in her chair and pose her legs at a sexy slant in order to give him a better picture of whatever it was he seemed to be searching for.

"He must not be such a hot lover, Mrs. Dunbar, because you're still prickly as a small porcupine. If you'd been in my keep for an entire weekend, there would be a sparkle in those blue eyes and a rosy glow in your cheeks."

That was too much for Abby to take. She slammed the file down, braced her fists on the edge of the desk, and glared at him. "He's an excellent lover, Mr. Weston, and I found him to be exactly what I needed and wanted. However, if I'd known you were so interested in every little detail of what occurred, I would have borrowed the office tape recorder and recorded each and every event."

Clint did not leave, as she'd hoped he would, but his expression turned chilly, and his eyes became dark and stormy. "You need a man to make love to you, Abby, not the fumbling unsureness of a boy." He came to his feet, his gaze never leaving her. "Be ready to leave in an hour."

After watching his long stride eat up the distance to his office and waiting until the door was tightly closed, Abby got up and hurried from the room.

She found Laura in the small, fully equipped lounge behind the reception room and wasted precious little time in informing her friend that their boss was a first-class bastard.

"What's the problem?" Laura asked, unperturbed, as she held a styrofoam cup beneath the coffee dispenser.

"Just where would you like for me to start?" Abby threw over her shoulder without interrupting her pacing. "I've had it up to here." She placed one hand flat against her chin. "It's become uncomfortable as hell, wondering what he's going to say or do next."

"What exactly did he do or say this morning?"

Abby related what had taken place, then stared disbelievingly as her friend laughed. "Have I missed something? Does having my personal life hashed and rehashed each morning by my employer come with the job?"

"I'm sorry," Laura managed to say as she struggled to get herself under control. She patted Abby reassuringly on the shoulder, then sat down at the tiny round table in the center of the small cubicle. "If you weren't so involved, you'd see the humor as well. Clint's acting totally out of character and, in so doing, has caused you to do and say things that a month ago would have caused you to blush at even the thought."

"And that's supposed to make me quiver with excitement?" Abby demanded. Damn it! She was mad. She'd had enough of Clint Weston and his underhanded remarks to last her a lifetime. The next time, the very next time he attacked her, she was going to pick up the heaviest object she could manage and bash it over his head.

"No," Laura said soothingly, "it's not. But James and I both have told you how to handle

53

him. Stand up to him. Tell him to go to hell. Tell him if he doesn't shape up, you'll quit. Whatever happens to come to mind.''

"I should think an employee who said such things to her boss would be begging to find a pink slip in her pay envelope," Abby retorted stonily.

"Clint is not the Major or Leon, Abby," Laura told her. "At the risk of insulting your father, I'd like to point out that having strength doesn't necessarily mean a man can't be fair. Clint would much rather have you return his yelling and his jabs than withdraw into a shell when you're around him. He's not the sort of individual to fire you just because you tell him to go jump in the lake."

"I'm trying to learn to cope with him, and I will," Abby declared. "But it isn't easy, believe me. I've never met a man who could make my blood boil by simply walking into the room."

Some forty-five minutes later Abby picked up the small cassette recorder and slipped it into the slim briefcase she carried on her outings with her boss. At that same moment Clint stepped through the door of his office.

She quickly changed her expression to one of casual interest, hoping he hadn't perceived the slight surge of panic that assailed her each time he appeared. She had changed from the taupe-colored heels into a pair of gray boots. Folded over one arm was a red thigh-length raincoat with a hood.

"Are you ready?" he asked after pausing and letting his gaze flow over her.

"Ready," Abby murmured, determined not to look away from him. Apparently whatever gods ruled her destiny had seen fit to place this large, intimidating man directly in her path. She could conquer him, or she could run and hide. *But,* she thought as she met his enigmatical stare, *I've taken the easy way out too many times. I think the moment has arrived for me to take a stand. So, if it's a fight you want, Mr. Weston, then it's a fight you'll get.*

CHAPTER FOUR

Conversation, once they were in the four-wheel-drive vehicle and on their way, ranged from sporadic to none at all, which suited Abby just fine. She'd yet to learn how to have a conversation with Clint without its turning into a battle. Besides, as she stared at the scenery flashing by, her thoughts were on seeing her father for dinner later in the evening, and she'd been racking her brain in an effort to come up with something tasty that wouldn't require hours in the kitchen.

Give him a sandwich and a bowl of soup, a tiny voice whispered wickedly, and Abby smiled as she imagined how insulted her parent would be by such treatment. Dinner to the Major was an affair where, in days past, his wife, then later a housekeeper and for a while Abby, prepared attractive as well as delicious dishes for him, then waited nervously for his approval.

Unfortunately for the Major the last time he had dined with his daughter at her place, he'd been treated to a very hastily thrown together tuna casserole, a green salad, and French bread. He'd eyed the fare rather haughtily, a fact Abby blithely ignored, and showed his annoyance that there was only fruit and cheese for dessert by drawing his lips together in a thin, disapproving line.

Suddenly a brilliant idea hit Abby. Why not introduce her father to Hamburger Helper? She was positive he had never tasted that particular culinary discovery. She would, however, soften the blow to his ego by making some sort of dessert. A smile tugged at her lips as she imagined his reaction, running the gamut from absolute incredulity to outraged disbelief.

"Have I missed something along the way?" the stern-featured Clint asked as he favored her with one of his curious glances.

"Not that I know of," Abby replied pleasantly, turning her head and meeting his frosty gaze.

"Then may I ask what you find so amusing?" His voice was less stern than it had been a moment ago. "I've never considered the scenery along this particular stretch of highway as one of the most hilarious sights in the world."

"Mmmm . . . For once I agree with you," Abby said softly.

"And you aren't going to tell me what brought that funny little smile to your lips, are you?"

"My thoughts are hardly top secret." She chuckled, for once not minding his prying. "Actually I was thinking about what I would serve my dinner guest this evening."

"Cal Densen must be special," Clint remarked. "But don't you think you're overdoing it a little? I mean, you've only known the man for less than a week."

"Cal *is* special," Abby answered with a perfectly straight face. "As for overdoing it . . ." She shrugged. "What can I say? When two people hit it off as perfectly as we did, it seems silly to hold back. Life is too short to let yourself be hampered by convention."

"Convention or not, intimate little dinners at a woman's apartment usually mean that an affair, if not already going on, isn't far off."

"And to think I owe all it all to you," Abby said innocently.

"What the hell is that supposed to mean?"

"Now, Mr. Weston, you mustn't be so modest," she said as earnestly as the suppressed laughter within her throat would allow. "Without you constantly nagging me to go out more, I'm afraid I'd never have met Cal."

Clint's reaction to this reminder of his interest in his employee caused him to clamp his teeth together so tightly, Abby was positive that at any second she would hear the grinding of his pearly whites. After a moment or two had passed, he sent her a chilly glance. "As I've mentioned before, I would prefer it if you'd call me Clint. Mr. Weston seems rather formal, considering how closely we work together."

"Whatever you say—Clint," Abby replied in her most professional voice. She was almost tempted to tell him that her guest for dinner would be her father and not Cal. But he was such a pain in the buns, constantly advising her on how to run her life and now simply assuming that she and Cal were having an affair. Perhaps if she were to let him think she was interested in another man, he would turn his obnoxious attention toward someone else.

Funny, she thought amusedly as she turned back to stare out the window, *four weeks ago I was in greater awe of Clint Weston than a child is of Santa Claus. Now here I sit, calmly accepting the fact that he thinks I'm sleeping with a man I've only known for four days. You're moving right along, Abby dear,* she congratulated herself, *moving right along.*

She couldn't help but wonder, though, just why Clint became angry each time Cal's name came up. According to her *charming* boss, her seeing another man was his own handiwork.

When they reached the construction site, Abby eyed with misgivings the steady drizzle of rain that had begun to fall in the last hour. Tramping around acres and acres of ground with all sorts of muck and litter making one afraid to take the next step wasn't her idea of a fun morning. She could well imagine the condition her hair would be in when they finished. She quickly slipped into the raincoat she'd brought along, tucked the briefcase and her purse beneath her arm, then opened the door and stepped out of the Ford Bronco. "Can I help you with anything?" Clint asked as he quickly stepped to her side.

"No, thanks." Abby smiled. "On second thought, you could see what you can do about this rain. When I left my apartment this morning, the sun was shining. Now it looks like the day is ruined."

"Not unless you and young Cal were planning a moonlight picnic this evening," he said mockingly, then placed a hand at her elbow and began hurrying her forward. "Otherwise, look upon the inclement weather as a good omen. There's something about a cool, rainy evening that makes two people want to cuddle."

Abby refrained from pointing out that she doubted the Major had ever cuddled with anyone, rainy or sunny. But the identity of her dinner guest was her own little secret, and she planned to keep it that way. Besides, she'd learned already that the less Clint knew about her personal life, the better it was for her. She'd never encountered a man so openly curious about another person's affairs. Nothing seemed too brazen for him to ask her. Little by little she was learning how to protect herself from his insatiable curiosity.

Abby was so busy patting herself on the back for her progress in the art of self-preservation that she failed to see the root that had been uncovered and left directly in the strewn path to the superintendent's mobile office. Her next step, however, hurriedly acquainted her with the object, when the toe of her boot became wedged beneath it.

One second she was upright, the next she was viewing at close range the muddy surface of Mother Earth, her briefcase and purse falling, then sliding at least two feet in front of her.

"What the hell happened?" Clint asked, astonished, as he quickly bent down and slipped his hands beneath her arms and lifted her to her feet. "I only took my hand off you for a second. Are you hurt?" His face showed concern.

"Hell, yes, I'm hurt!" Abby stormed at him. Though to be truthful, she was hard pressed to decide which was worse, the injury to her pride or the stinging abrasions on her knees and palms.

Clint oddly avoided making eye contact with her and began to wipe at her injuries with his handkerchief. The reason for this reluctance became obvious to Abby when she saw the suspicious trembling of his lips as he tried not to laugh.

"Give me that!" She reached out and snatched the once white square of linen from him and began dabbing at her hands, wincing when she came into contact with a deep scratch on one palm. "I don't need a conceited jackass waving a handkerchief about while he's laughing at me."

"Yes, ma'am," Clint said solemnly, his gray eyes brimming with laughter. He walked over and picked up the purse and briefcase, holding each between a careful thumb and forefinger. "I'm afraid we'll need more than a handkerchief for these."

"Well, I'm sure there's a washroom in Jack's trailer. Would you mind carrying them for me, or will it throw you into another fit of hysterics?" She glared at him.

"I think I can manage it." He looked down at her from his towering height, his expression so bland that Abby was tempted to kick him. "But you'll be needing a great deal more than Jack's washroom. There's blood on one knee, your panty hose are ruined, your skirt is dirty, your hands are scraped, and your face looks like you've been making mud pies."

"Thank you so much for your very thorough review of my appearance, Mr. Weston. Now if you'll excuse me, I think I'll go see Jack. Why don't you go brighten someone else's day?"

That revolting ass! Abby silently cursed several minutes later as she squeezed warm water from the washcloth and tried to clean the grime from the long scratch on her knee. He'd actually had the nerve to laugh at her. Uncaring that she might have broken an ankle or sprained her wrist, he'd stood, like the flaming idiot she knew him to be, and laughed at her. "I'll fix him," she muttered to herself. "One of these days I'll catch him in a tight spot, and when I do"—she pursed her lips wickedly—"I'll make him rue the day he was so thoughtless." After tidying up the tiny bathroom she hobbled into the office area of the trailer.

Jack Meirs opened the first-aid kit and removed a bottle of disinfectant, a roll of gauze, some adhesive tape, and a tube of cream. "You'd better be liberal with the disinfectant, Abby," he told her. "That's a pretty mean-looking cut on your knee."

"Thanks, Jack." She smiled, then grimaced when she uncapped the bottle and got a good whiff of the medication. "What on earth is this?"

"Essence of horse liniment." The tall blond-headed man grinned. "A good application of that"—he nodded toward the odoriferous liquid

—"and you'll be surprised at how uncrowded your life will become for a number of hours."

Abby regarded the bottle for several seconds, then recapped it and set it on the table. "I think I'll stick with the antibacterial cream."

"Chicken," Jack softly taunted with a chuckle. He replaced the antiseptic in the first-aid kit. "Seriously, though, I would get a tetanus shot when I got back to town if I were you. At one time several acres of this land were used for dumping." After Abby applied a light coating of cream to a large square of gauze, he took the bandage and placed it over the cut on her knee—just as Clint opened the door and entered the trailer.

Abby met his flinty-eyed stare as he took in Jack bending solicitously over her, his large hands carefully taping the bandage in place, and almost laughed at the look of displeasure that distorted his features.

"When you get through playing doctor, Jack, I would like to see the blueprints for that last storage tank they're installing." Clint spoke in what Abby had come to think of as his I'm-itching-for-a-fight voice.

Apparently Jack was well aware of his boss's moods as well, for he flashed Abby a grin of amusement, then straightened and walked over to a double row of file cabinets.

And though her anger had cooled considerably and she no longer had a desire to part his skull, Abby blithely ignored Clint. If he wanted to act like a horse's behind, then she would treat him like one. She calmly inspected the scrapes on her palms and applied the same treatment to them as she had her knees. The large bandages would be bulky, and the skin was burning like crazy.

After several minutes of being ignored Clint walked over to where she was sitting. "I'll take you to your apartment when we leave here, and you can take the rest of the day off."

"Thank you," Abby said quietly. "I would like to change clothes, but I don't think it's necessary for me to take time off."

"As you wish," he said curtly, then swung around to take a look at the blueprint Jack was spreading out on a drafting table.

Except for a request from Clint for the small tape recorder, conversation between Abby and her boss amounted to zero during the time he and Jack spent poring over the blueprint. Clint was obviously upset about some aspect of the construction of the storage tanks, and he wasn't content until he'd found the mistake and pointed it out to the superintendent.

Once that problem was out of the way, he came back to where Abby was sitting. Without asking her permission he slipped his hands beneath her elbows. "Do you think you can walk, or would you rather I carried you?" he asked in a gruff voice.

I'd rather crawl than be carried in your arms, she was tempted to tell him. But a hasty consideration of the probable repercussions of such a reply brought forth a more amiable response. "I'm sure I'll be able to manage," she said, and then gasped in pain when, forgetting her sore hands, she placed one palm on the surface of the desk to brace herself.

Before she realized what he was doing, Clint had bent forward and slipped one arm beneath her shoulders and the other beneath her knees and swung her up to his chest. An amused Jack picked up her briefcase and purse, held open the door, then followed them to the Bronco.

"Remember to get that shot," he reminded Abby after she was safely in the front seat and Clint was getting in on the driver's side.

"Don't worry, I will." She smiled up at him. "You've been very kind, Jack, th—"

The sentence was never finished. Clint started the engine and jammed his foot on the accelerator with such force, they were halfway across the large tract of land before Abby could catch her surprised breath.

She swung around to face the scowling man behind the wheel, her lips tight with disapproval. "*Must* you be so rude?" she came near to shouting.

"*Must* you flirt like a fifteen-year-old with my construction supervisor?" Clint shot right back.

"Flirt?" Abby cried disbelievingly. "You call thanking someone for helping you flirting?"

"When the lady in question flutters her eyelashes like a damned hummingbird hovering over a flower and smiles the way you were doing, I sure as hell do call it flirting," he threw at her.

"Well, this may come as a surprise to you, Mr. Weston, but even if I had been acting as you just described, which I wasn't, what business is it of

65

yours?" she asked challengingly. She was so outraged by the unfair accusation, she felt as though each individual hair on her head was standing on end. The nerve of him!

"It's simple, Mrs. Dunbar. When you're on my time, I expect you to conduct yourself in a manner befitting your age and position. You can play the vamp after five."

"My age and position?" she asked, astonished. "My God! You make me sound as though I'm one year from Social Security. As for my position, you can take it and go straight to hell. I resign." She fell back against the seat and crossed her arms over her heaving bosom. This was the last straw, the very last straw. She'd endured his nosy prying into her personal life and his insufferable remarks regarding her social activities. But taking her to task for failing to act in a manner befitting her age and position was the limit.

For a moment Clint imagined the steering wheel his large hands were gripping was Jack Meirs's throat. When he'd walked into that trailer and found Abby and Jack smiling and talking to each other, he'd seen red. She hadn't wanted him to touch her, but a virtual stranger was treated like an old friend.

He shot a quick glance at the stubborn set of his passenger's chin as she stared straight ahead. "I refuse to accept your resignation, Mrs. Dunbar," he said quietly but determinedly. "You and I have a contractual agreement, which you signed and which I have in my files. According to that contract only I have the right to terminate our association."

Abby slowly turned her head, her eyes dark and stormy as she stared at him. "Sue me."

"If you aren't at your desk by eight thirty tomorrow morning, that is exactly what I will do." Clint glared at her.

Why the hell, of all the women he knew, was he letting Abby Dunbar get to him? She certainly wasn't the most beautiful he'd known, nor the most cooperative, he grimly reflected. Yet there was something about her that had caught his eye that first day and which continued to affect him powerfully.

He'd also seen, in the short time she had been working for him, a slow but steadily developing maturity emerging in her. In his mind's eye he went back over the first few days of Abby's employment with Weston, Inc. She'd been shy, almost afraid to breathe in his presence. But as the days wore on Clint had seen her shyness disappear and a certain gutsy determination begin to surface. He was inordinately curious about her, finding it difficult to believe that in this day and age a woman could be as intimidated as she was. He'd studied her file but found nothing that gave him a clue about the real Abby Dunbar.

As he approached the street where she lived he broke the stony silence that had prevailed for the last few miles. "I'm afraid you'll have to direct me. I remember the street, but not the number."

Abby gave him the information in as few words as possible, then placed her fingers in readiness on the door handle. As soon as they came to a complete stop, she pulled at the lever, but nothing happened. She tried again, and still the door didn't open. With a mutinous expression on her face Abby turned and stared at Clint. "Will you please stop playing games and unlock this door?"

"Why, certainly, Abby," Clint said pleasantly, as though they'd been on a nice leisurely drive, and ignoring the fact that she was glaring at him with murder in her eyes. "And, yes, I'd be delighted to come in and have a cup of coffee." He smiled at her as he opened his door and got out.

"Then why don't you go down two blocks, hang a right, then a left, and you'll find yourself at a nice little restaurant," she replied stonily as he opened her door and offered her his hand.

Abby would have liked nothing better in the world than to ignore his gallant gesture, but her knees felt stiff as two boards.

"I'd rather have coffee with you—in your apartment, Abby." He slid one arm around her waist, cupped her elbow with his other hand, then ushered her toward her door. "Don't worry about being the perfect hostess. I'll take care of everything while you have a nice warm shower," he told her with a perfectly straight face.

"Believe me, acting as hostess to you, perfect or otherwise, is the last thing on my mind. I don't want you in my apartment, and I don't want any coffee," Abby told him as they reached her door.

"My, my," Clint murmured in mock sympathy. "Perhaps if we had invited Jack Meirs, you would have felt more hospitable. We might even give handsome Cal a call. Would that make a few minutes in my presence, outside of our employer-employee relationship, more palatable?"

"I do believe there's sawdust in your head instead of a brain," Abby flung at him. With trembling hands she jerked open her purse, removed the key, and unlocked the door. She dropped her purse without even looking to see where it landed, then stalked across the room in the direction of the hallway. "Make yourself at home," she remarked facetiously over her shoulder.

The water stung like the very devil as it came into contact with the marks on her skin. But, Abby reasoned with her jaw set grimly, her physical discomfort was nothing compared to the anger she was feeling. Damn Clint Weston! He'd laughed at her, accused her of having an affair with a man she barely knew, implied she was making a play for one of his employees, and lastly had barged his way into her apartment, where he knew he wasn't welcome. Just how important was her damn job?

But you've resigned, a tiny smug voice whispered as she turned off the shower, then reached for a towel. *You don't have to worry about your job. No, I don't,* she thought maliciously, *and Mr. Weston can very well get the hell out of my apartment.*

Never had Abby dressed so fast. Her hands literally flew as they grabbed fresh underwear and panty hose from a drawer. She jerked a beige silk blouse and a tan skirt from their hangers and threw them on, stepped into a pair of taupe pumps, then hastily checked her makeup and hair. There was nothing but revenge glittering in her eyes as she opened the door of her bedroom and barreled through it like a shot out of a cannon.

She found the object of her thoughts prowling about her living room, one hand holding a mug of steaming coffee, the other tucked finger-deep in the back pocket of his pants.

On hearing her rather abrupt entrance into the room, Clint turned, his gray-eyed gaze sweeping over her. His eyes narrowed, and his expression was unreadable as he took in the commanding stance of her small body and the hostility emanating from her.

"I like this room, Abby," he said finally. "It reflects the warmth of the person who lives here."

"Thank you," she said stiffly. She moved into the room, her hands tightly clenched at her sides. This wasn't going at all the way she'd planned. But there was no way he was going to put her off with a few meaningless compliments. "Now that you've had your coffee, would you mind leaving?"

Instead of doing as she asked, however, Clint began to close the distance between them, his long strides eating up the space with incredible swiftness—or so it seemed to Abby, who watched his approach with a mixture of alarm and uncertainty.

"I'm not accustomed to having a woman treat me as though I'm a carrier of the plague," he said softly, stopping directly in front of her. Without taking his eyes off her face he set the mug of coffee on the square table at the end of the sofa, and then, before she could step back, let his hands slowly slide up her silk-clad arms to her shoulders. "What is there about me, Abby, that causes you to want to run and hide when we're alone?"

"I—I'm sure you're imagining things," she said in a voice she barely recognized as her own. His fingers were moving against the tense muscles of her shoulders in tiny but electrifying circles that left miniature darts of fire in their wake.

"Am I?" he murmured. "Since I'm the kind of man who likes to know what's what, let's see who's right, shall we?"

The hands that had been creating such an exciting warmth with their touch now moved over her back from shoulder to waist and at the same time drew her to him with such subtle force that Abby was unaware of it until she felt the firm tips of her breasts come into contact with the hardness of his chest.

She raised her hands to push him back, her body's protective reflexes coming to life even though her senses had suddenly taken a leave of absence. This wasn't what she'd intended when she'd envisioned a showdown with Clint, she thought frantically, her eyes fixed on the sensuous curve of his lips and the deep cleft in his chin, which were coming closer and closer. She should be basking in her moment of glory for having thrown him out of her apartment instead of standing like a statue in his arms.

On the other hand, she thought dazedly as she felt the first touch of his mouth against hers, statues weren't supposed to have feeling, were they? They couldn't know the tiny shivers of awakening that could be caused by the feather light stroke of a tongue tracing the outline of their lifeless lips. But Abby did. She felt the urgent but gentle pressure as Clint demanded admittance to the secrets of her mouth. As though on command, she granted him that entry, then became dizzy with sensations she wasn't ready to put a name to as his tongue swirled around hers in an erotic dance that was a prelude to a deeper and more satisfying union between a man and a woman.

He gave and she took, her hands clutching at his shoulders for support as her knees threatened to give out from under her. His face and name became blurred as need and desire awakened and began their journey throughout her limbs. As though it had a will of its own, her body moved enticingly against the hands that were stroking and working their way over her hips and along the forgotten points of arousal along her spine.

When the lips that had stirred the slumbering fires of passion within her left her mouth and sought the soft pink tip of one ear, then pressed against the wildly beating pulse in her throat, Abby heard a faint groan of protest slip past her lips. This was her own personal pleasure, and she wanted nothing to interfere with it; yet something she could not fathom stopped her from taking it.

She was brought back to reality by two large hands cupping her face and a deep, soft voice demanding that she open her eyes.

"Look at me, Abby," Clint said in a near whisper.

"If it's all the same with you, I'd rather not," she replied. All she wanted was to be left alone— to be allowed to go into some quiet corner and ponder the whys and wherefores of what had happened.

But Clint's low chuckle brought her eyes open, and she stared into his gaze. "Don't look so triumphant," she remarked crossly.

"Ah, no, Abby." He smiled tenderly. "Not triumphant. I'm shocked, right down to my very toes."

"Shocked?" she asked querulously. "Aren't women of my *age and position* allowed to enjoy an occasional kiss?"

"Oh, indeed, yes." Clint grinned. "And I intend to see that in the future you are accorded that opportunity on a regular basis. Have dinner with me this evening."

You ass! One kiss and you think you are the answer to this widow's prayers, Abby silently raged. "Sorry." She smiled. "I already have a date for this evening. Did you forget?"

"Break it." Clint uttered the two words in his best boardroom voice.

"I don't break dates," she said evenly. "Besides, being a widow with limited *opportunities,* I find I

73

must take advantage of each one that comes my way."

For one brief second she thought she had pushed Clint too far. His hands, which had dropped to her shoulders, tightened in a painful grip, his face dark with fury. "Cal Densen is a boy, Abby, and a boy is not what you need. You're aching for a man to make love to you. Don't mistake the two."

"And you think you're that man?" she asked with a hint of derision in her voice, wondering where on earth she had found the courage to have this remarkable conversation.

"I don't think, sweetheart, I *know* I am. And so will you before it's over." He dropped his hands to his sides and stepped back. "Get your purse, and I'll take you back to the office if you wish. But my offer for the afternoon off still stands if you think you need it."

CHAPTER FIVE

Abby roared out of the parking lot of Weston, Inc., her mind in a tailspin. *Of all the men you might have gone into a heavy clench with, why did you have to choose Clint Weston?* she asked herself. It wasn't the deed itself that was causing her problems. She wasn't a cold person, and there had been occasions before her marriage to Corey and since his death when a kiss had been more than a casual peck on the lips. But her response to Clint had been something totally unexpected, leaving her on edge. It was as though he'd opened a door to her emotions and allowed a whirlwind to enter.

With a superhuman effort she tried to put the feel and touch of him out of her mind. There were more pressing problems facing her, mainly the one of whether or not she wanted to continue working for him. She'd said in anger that she was resigning, but did she really want to do that? *No, you don't,* that inner voice she was beginning to hate told her. *His eternal sniping made you feel inadequate, and you were merely retaliating. You know you like the job. And if you're honest with yourself, you'll admit that you're beginning to get some sort of curious thrill from the continual sparring the two of you indulge in, not to mention the physical attraction you know is there— regardless of how heatedly you deny it.*

With a muttered groan of disgust for allowing a man with characteristics remarkably like those of her father to occupy her thoughts, Abby forced herself to concentrate on the shopping she needed to do for dinner after she got the tetanus shot from her doctor. Her most recent clash with Clint as well her own streak of pure cussedness had reinforced her determination not to spend hours in the kitchen. Perhaps it was time for the Major to learn, much to his regret, she was sure, that the world didn't revolve around his wants and needs. He would be served a simple meal, and he would damn well like it, Abby promised herself as she flipped on the left-hand turn signal and whipped into a parking spot in front of her doctor's office.

Several hours later the kitchen was filled with the tempting aroma of noodles stroganoff. There was steamed broccoli with cheese sauce, plus a green salad waiting in the fridge. Abby was dotting the dinner rolls with butter when the door-bell sounded. She wiped her hands on a tea towel and hurried to open the door.

"You're right on time." She smiled at her still handsome father, then stood on her tiptoes and kissed him on the cheek. He'd dressed casually in a dark blue knit shirt and matching pants, the color going well with the salt-and-pepper color of his hair.

"Of course I am," he replied in a halfway shocked voice. "I detest people who aren't punctual." He stepped inside and closed the door. "I hope you have something decent in your liquor cabinet. I need a drink."

Old habits die hard, and at his mention of a drink Abby's first inclination was to rush to the kitchen and mix his usual scotch and water. Instead she said, "I haven't had time to check my supply since you were here last, so I'm afraid you'll have to make do with what you can find." She turned and headed for the kitchen. "And while you're making yours, how about fixing me a rum and Coke?" She threw over her shoulder.

John Ransom stared disbelievingly at the retreating back of his daughter, his mouth hanging open as though he had received the shock of his life—a sight Abby would have given her eyeteeth to have witnessed. After recovering from this heretofore unheard of treatment, however, he went along to the kitchen and asked in an icy voice where she kept the liquor and glasses.

Abby, carefully arranging her features in a mask of pleasantness, told him, then took the salad from the fridge and began filling two individual bowls. "How was your day?" she asked cheerfully, knowing from experience that there was nothing her father liked better than to talk about his job. He lived and breathed the military.

That artful maneuver on her part broke the ice and helped the Major overcome his annoyance at having to actually mix his own drink. His recital of the incidents of the day lasted until they were nearly finished with the main course, when he abruptly changed the subject by complimenting her on the noodles stroganoff.

"This must have taken hours to prepare," he remarked as he took a sip of wine. "I'm surprised you were able to take time off from this job you seem to be so fond of."

"Oh, there was no reason to ask for time off to throw this meal together." She smiled pleasantly at her father across the table. "It's nothing more illustrious than Hamburger Helper, Dad. You should try it sometime. It takes less than an hour to prepare, and as you said, it tastes delicious."

Twice in one evening John Ransom had been thrown off stride. He looked from his daughter to the food on his plate, then smiled thinly. "Perhaps the next time I come for dinner you will have gotten over this foolish notion you have of becoming a career woman and will have time to cook a meal the way you were taught to do."

"Gee, I doubt it, Dad." Abby pretended to be giving the idea considerable thought. "I'm really beginning to get the hang of things in my job. Quite frankly I could never go back to being the way I once was. I like having a career. It gives me a feeling of self-worth, of being in control of my life. I like that."

"Which you could have just as easily if you'd give up this ridiculous apartment and job and move back in with me. I'd much prefer having my daughter run my home than a housekeeper."

"That's very sweet of you, Dad, but housekeeping isn't very challenging. Nor is it what I want to do with my life. Why don't you get married?"

Whatever his answer to her question would have been, Abby never knew. For at that moment the doorbell rang. She murmured "Excuse me" to the grim-faced major and offered up a silent prayer of thanks for the reprieve from what was fast becoming an unpleasant conversation.

When she opened the door, though, Abby wasn't sure which was the lesser of the two evils, her father waiting in the dining alcove or Clint Weston waiting to be invited in.

For several seconds she simply stared at him casually leaning against her doorframe. What on earth could he possibly want? And then it dawned on her. Of course, her rat of a boss was up to his usual snooping. He'd erroneously assumed Cal would be here and had stopped in to ruin what he thought would be a tender, intimate evening.

"Hello, Abby." He smiled lazily, his teasing eyes lingering on her slightly parted lips, then running over the fullness of her small breasts beneath the pink V-necked crocheted top she was wearing with white slacks.

Abby endured this open appraisal of her body with a sense of resignation. Letting him see her resentment would only bring on something even more outrageous. "Clint," she murmured, "what can I do for you?" Then mentally kicked herself for asking such a stupid question, considering how easily he twisted everything she said.

"I was in the neighborhood," he said brazenly, "and thought I'd drop by and make sure you were recovering from your fall this morning. I also thought I'd say hello to Cal. Since I feel responsible for having urged you to get out more, I think it's my duty to make sure you're in safe hands."

"Your concern overwhelms me," Abby replied so sweetly he was taken aback. She reached out and caught hold of the sleeve of his jacket, then pulled him inside and closed the door. "I can't tell you what a relief it is to know there is someone like you looking after me, Clint," she said as she directed him through the living room and into the dining room.

Her father looked up, startled to see his daughter and a strange man enter the room. "I wasn't aware that you were expecting guests, Abby," he said reproachfully.

"Oh, but this isn't a friend, Major. This is my boss. Clint Weston, I'd like you to meet my good friend Major John Ransom," she said with a perfectly straight face.

It looked for a second as though the Major wasn't going to go along with the ruse, but after a quick glance at Abby and the dancing devils of mischief in her blue eyes, some tiny holdover from when he was young and not so exacting asserted itself. He reached over and clasped Clint's outstretched hand. "Mr. Weston," he said in a firm voice, "it's a pleasure to meet you."

Clint managed some response, though he wasn't exactly sure what it was. He sat down at

Abby's and the Major's bidding, and then, as he began to take in the looks and gestures of familiarity flowing between his hostess and her aging lothario, his expression slowly changed from one of dazed disbelief to one of cool remoteness.

This character was old enough to be Abby's father, Clint thought savagely as he tried to keep up with the conversation and the questions being asked him by the older man. What the hell was she thinking of, getting involved in a situation like this? This old coot made Cal Densen seem like Prince Charming, Clint decided, then immediately rejected that idea. Ransom was too old, and Densen was too young. Abby needed a man who was mature enough to cherish and protect her, but young enough to be a partner *with* her in life. *Watch it, Weston. You're reacting like an inexperienced man looking at life through rose-colored glasses*, a warning voice told him. *After two marriages, neither of which was exactly made in heaven, you should know better.*

But neither the cryptic proddings of his mind regarding his past forays into the realm of wedded bliss nor his reflections on his jaded past could wipe away the ugly taste in his mouth as he pictured Abby in the arms of John Ransom.

Dessert, which tasted like sawdust to Clint, came and went. And when, to his astonishment, the Major announced shortly afterward that he had another appointment and had to leave, Clint watched closely as Abby saw her dinner guest to the door. When the only show of affection between them was a chaste peck on the cheek, he

81

breathed a sigh of relief. Surely if they were more than casual friends, there would have been a more affectionate farewell than what he'd just seen.

Abby turned from closing the door on her father's departure and faced Clint, who had gotten up from the table and was leaning against the wall just inside the living room.

"How about another piece of apple pie?" she asked brightly, struggling to maintain an expression of polite unconcern. For once she was having the privilege of seeing her boss at a distinct disadvantage.

"I thought you said you were seeing Cal Densen this evening," Clint said accusingly, following her back to the table, where she began clearing away the dirty dishes.

"Correction." Abby smiled at him. "You assumed it was Cal. I never mentioned the name of the man I would be seeing this evening." She picked up the plates, with the flatware and salad bowls stacked on top, and turned toward the door of the kitchen. "What do you think of the Major?" she asked with a perfectly straight face.

"I think he's too damn old for you." Clint gathered up napkins, glasses, and dessert plates and followed her. "Even though you've been married, you're still incredibly naïve where men are concerned. The more I'm around you, the more I'm convinced your parents must have arranged your marriage."

"What on earth makes you think that?" Abby asked, mildly curious. She opened the dishwasher and began stacking the dishes on the rack, thinking as she did how close to the truth he really was. Aside from the fact that he was not a military man, the mild-mannered Corey had suited her father perfectly. The Major would never have welcomed an outspoken, independent son-in-law.

"Because it's obvious you know nothing about men." Clint frowned as he leaned against the counter and watched her. "One minute you're raving about Cal Densen, and the next thing I see is you having a cozy dinner with a man old enough to be your father."

"Then perhaps you'll approve of Julian." She turned and smiled pleasantly at him.

"Who the hell is Julian?" he asked in a rough voice.

"A—friend." Abby shrugged. She began tidying up the counter, then looked questioningly at Clint. "More coffee and pie?"

"Coffee please, but no more pie," he said in a harassed manner. "Tell me more about this Julian character. Exactly what does he do?" Lord! he thought explosively. Just how damn many men did she know?

Abby smiled as she got down cups and saucers and set them on a tray, then filled each with coffee. "Why don't you carry this into the living room while I finish up in here?" she asked. "I'll only be a minute." With reluctance plainly showing on his face Clint did as she asked.

In the few minutes it took for her to put the small kitchen in order, Abby found that she was enjoying the evening. She certainly hadn't planned on playing what had turned out to be a very neat trick on Clint. Once the whole thing started, however, her sense of humor—and a tiny bit of desire for revenge—took over.

As for the occasional pangs of guilt she experienced as she hurried through her chores, she promptly dismissed them. From the first day she had been on his payroll, she reminded herself, Clint had taken it upon himself to "redo" her. He'd assumed, in that high and mighty, know-it-all manner, that she was a poor, frightened widow, staring at life like a child through a candy store window.

But she'd be the first to admit her life had changed and was finally beginning to go in a direction of her own choosing. And she resented Clint's assuming he had carte blanche to push, twist, or turn her in any direction he chose. There was a decided gleam in her blue eyes as she turned and switched off the light, then went to join her waiting guest.

She found him sitting on the edge of the sofa, his elbows braced on his knees, his hands loosely clasped. He appeared to be staring thoughtfully into space. It was only when she was further into the room that she saw the reason for his rapt concentration.

"Is that a photograph of your husband?" Clint asked, pulling his gaze from the smiling face of Corey to watch Abby as she sat down on the sofa.

"Yes." She smiled gently, her eyes going to the photograph, then back to Clint. "That was taken during a short vacation the first summer we were married. I'm surprised you didn't notice it earlier today."

Clint leaned back, his enigmatic expression revealing nothing. "What line of work was he in, Abby? In all our discussions I don't recall you ever mentioning that."

That's because you've been too busy painting me as a gray mouse, she was tempted to tell him. "Corey was associated with his older brother, who is an investment broker. I'm sure you've heard of the firm—Shute, Dunbar, and Kettering."

He frowned thoughtfully. "Ah, yes. I've never done business with them, but from all accounts they're a very solid organization. Was Corey a partner?"

Again Abby smiled. "No, Corey wasn't a partner. He was given some nondescript title that kept him from being a source of embarrassment to his brother. Frankly, my husband was a dreamer. I think at one time in his life he would have liked to be a musician, but his brother, Leon, decided that wasn't a fitting career. So Corey bowed to his wishes and did as he was told."

"Didn't it ever occur to him to strike out on his own?" Clint asked curiously.

"As you would have done?" Abby thoughtfully regarded the large man seated beside her, having no difficulty at all imagining the stir he would have caused if someone such as Leon had tried to run his life. Knowing him as she did, she was quite certain Clint would have become tops in whatever field he chose. He was a fighter—a winner. On the one hand, she admired him for his strength and tenacity. On the other, she resented those same qualities in him, resented him for having been graced with them in such abundance while Corey had been so sadly shortchanged with respect to those strengths. "This may come as a complete surprise to you, Clint, but there are people born into this world who can't run huge corporations, who can't become President or world leaders. They simply want to find their own little niche in the scheme of life and live peacefully and happily."

"Is that what Corey wanted?"

"I think so. But by the time I met him he'd been so indoctrinated by Leon, he'd lost his inner resolve to be his own person."

Clint was silent for several seconds, then leaned forward and reached for a cup of the waiting coffee. "Who is Julian?" The question, though not totally unexpected, caught Abby by surprise.

"A sculptor friend of mine," she said unhesitatingly.

"Are you seeing him as well as Densen and this Major Ransom character?" he asked bitingly.

"Of course. I took your advice to come out of my shell very seriously. Don't you approve?"

Without having tasted the coffee Clint replaced the cup and saucer on the tray. He then turned toward Abby and placed his hands on her shoulders so swiftly that she was momentarily taken aback. "I think we can dispense with this little game of you pretending to be a shy, retiring widow, don't you?" he said with a harshness that sent a shiver of warning to her brain.

"I have no idea what you're talking about," Abby said shakily. She raised her hands and placed them against his chest in a gesture intended to keep him away, a gesture that proved as useless as a fluttering leaf against the strength of the wind when he suddenly pulled her to him. It was one thing to play games with Clint when he stayed at a safe distance. Suddenly finding herself in his arms added a new dimension to the game, one she wasn't quite sure how to handle.

"Oh, I think you do know what I'm talking about, Abby," he said huskily, his eyes sweeping lazily over her flushed features. "Just how far were you planning on carrying this little charade, hmmm?"

"Er—charade?" she parroted. This incredible scene was remarkably familiar, she thought as she focused her attention on his lips and the river of desire swirling beneath the dam of her defenses, waiting—yearning—for his touch to open the floodgates.

Clint's soft, gentle chuckle broke through her quiet, desperate reverie and caused Abby to raise concerned blue eyes to meet his unreadable gray ones. After staring intently at her for several seconds he gave a sharp shake of his dark head. "You are a mass of contradictions, Abby Dunbar, but for some strange reason I don't mind at all. You keep pretending, if that makes you feel better, and I'll keep digging until I find what it is about you that fascinates me so. In the meantime I think the taste of your lips will help me considerably in my investigation."

Abby didn't even try to evade his mouth as it moved with swift certainty to capture hers. There was no gentleness in him this time. It was as though each and every disagreement they'd had in their short acquaintance was remembered and his lips were meting out punishment. But instead of hurting, Abby found herself eagerly accepting the caress of his tongue against hers as she rode, for the second time that day, the crest of the wave of excitement this overbearing man seemed so capable of creating in her.

When one large hand stole beneath the edge of her sweater and snaked its way upward and cupped the fullness of one breast, Abby felt some of the well-being surrounding her begin to fade. She was already aware, from her two brief encounters with Clint in the role of lover, that if caution was to be exercised, then it would best be done quickly and firmly.

Sensing her withdrawal, Clint raised his head and stared down at her. "Playing hard to get, Abby?"

Feigning a nonchalance that was totally at odds with her entire being, she calmly returned his probing stare. "Is there some hard and fast rule that says I must allow you to set the tempo?"

A smile played about the corners of his mouth. "No rules, but it would probably prove to be very enjoyable for both of us if you would put yourself in my hands."

"Spoken like the true egotist you really are," Abby said without any real malice in her voice. "Unfortunately I happen not to be in the mood to put myself in your hands."

"Don't you trust me?" Clint had the audacity to ask.

"Trust has nothing to do with it." She grinned. "I'm simply not ready for an affair. It takes me longer to accept upheavals or changes in my life than most people."

"Do you have any idea just when you think you might be ready to let me make love to you?" Clint asked with a straight face, his eyes brimming with amusement.

"You? Aren't you being rather presumptuous? You're my boss, and I'm not sure I like the idea of your being my lover as well. Working conditions could become complicated, you know. But if and when I change my mind, I'll be sure to let you know."

"Do that." Clint chuckled. He picked up her hand and with one finger gently probed the edge of the scrape on the heel of her palm. He bent his head and pressed his lips against the tiny abrasion, then looked at Abby. "In the meantime, have dinner with me tomorrow evening— please?"

"I'd like that." The words of acceptance burst from her lips without the slightest effort. She'd meant to say no—to refuse. With the exception of the weekends they had been together every day since she'd started working for him. And when she wasn't with him, he was in her thoughts.

Now, after what had taken place today, there was no way in the world she was going to be able to maintain an objective attitude toward him. It seemed as though the more cautious she knew she should become, the more daring she actually became.

Without further arguing or attempting to take advantage of a situation in which he was fairly certain he could prevail, Clint rose to go. Abby, her feelings too new and disturbing to define, walked with him to the door.

"I won't be in the office until tomorrow afternoon, so if your knee is bothering you in the morning, why don't you sleep late?"

"Thanks, but I'm sure it will be all right," Abby said in an embarrassed voice, finding his concern almost as difficult to handle as his kisses.

Before she could guess his next move, Clint bent his head and brushed his lips against her forehead, then was gone. Abby stood for several seconds without moving, except for the fingers of one hand, the tips of which gently stroked the spot where his lips had touched her.

What, she asked herself, rather bemused, was she going to do with Clint Weston? She'd sworn that she hated him—but she didn't. She'd tried to ignore him—but she couldn't. She'd even threatened to resign—but she knew she wouldn't.

For some unaccountable reason her gaze fell on Corey's photograph. She stared at the familiar likeness for several soul-searching moments, then quietly walked over to the bookcase and picked up the silver frame. She held it carefully in her arms, cradled gently against her breasts. When she reached her bedroom, she took down a box from the shelf in the closet, opened it, and placed the photograph inside.

most couldn't be ... ...her ... ... When she ... ...ed her bedroom, she ... to ... her ...rm the ... on the closet ... did ... slam the closet with force.

CHAPTER SIX

The next morning found Abby at her desk at the usual time. It wasn't that she didn't appreciate Clint's offer of a few hours off; she did. But considering what had taken place between them the day before, she was more determined than ever to do her job well—without any special favors from the boss.

She was in the lounge having a cup of coffee with Laura when she got the expected phone call from the Major. She was surprised he hadn't awakened her at daylight demanding an explanation.

"Would you mind telling me what all that flimflam was about last night?" he asked briskly.

"Just a little trick I wanted to play on my boss," Abby told him, wishing he'd waited until she was back at her desk before calling. Explaining with Laura eavesdropping was embarrassing. "You played your part beautifully."

"Mmmm" was his only comment on the dubious compliment. "Is there something going on between you and this Weston fellow that I should know about?"

"No," Abby said slowly. "No, I don't think so.

He's—er—interesting to work for, and he pays well. In my short professional career I've learned that those two things take priority over all else."

"If you say so," the Major remarked dryly. "I have to hang up now. I have another call. Call me in a couple of days," he ordered in his usual authoritative tone of voice.

After she hung up, Abby turned to find a very curious Laura watching her. "Has something happened to upset the Major?"

"Oh, no." Abby tried to evade the issue. "He came over for dinner last night and was curious about something, that's all."

"I assume he mentioned something about Clint." Laura grinned wickedly. "Have the two of them met yet?"

"As a matter of fact," Abby said defeatedly, "they have—last night at my apartment."

"Ohhh! That must have been interesting. Tell me about it."

Abby stared at the blonde for several seconds, then shrugged. "Clint dropped by unexpectedly last night while the Major and I were having dinner. Naturally, being of a suspicious nature, he assumed the Major was my boyfriend."

"And of course you didn't bother to correct his mistaken impression?" Laura chuckled.

Abby smiled and tipped her head slightly forward. "You do know me so well, don't you?"

"What brought about this desire to play tricks on your boss?"

"It comes from my boss's poking his considerable nose into my business. He thought it was Cal

I was having over for dinner. When he walked in and saw the Major, you should have seen his face."

"I'm surprised old Ironpants went along with the deception."

"Frankly, so was I," Abby admitted. "But since he'd already received two severe shocks during the evening, I suppose he figured it wouldn't hurt him." She related his reactions to having to fix his own drink and then later to being told what he was eating.

It was several minutes before Laura could quit laughing after listening to the comical account of the evening. "I'm sorry I missed it," she remarked when she could speak again. "Did you ever tell Clint the truth?"

"And spoil all my fun? Of course not. Once he realized my social life wasn't the direct result of his timely intervention, I think he cast me in the role of a sexually deprived female—flitting from man to man like a butterfly."

"Do you still dislike him as intensely as you first did?" Laura asked curiously.

"Really, Laura." Abby frowned. "Must you know every thought that passes through my mind?"

"Only if you'll tell me," the receptionist candidly replied, her eyes sparkling mischievously. "Watching you and Clint is better than a soap opera. Besides, I happen to think the two of you would make a nice couple."

"A couple of what?" Abby asked, being deliberately obtuse.

Laura shrugged, her hands spread expressively. "Whatever comes to mind. You could team up as detectives, trapeze artists, Mr. and Mrs. Santa Claus, or you could have the affair of the century and end up with some really great memories to tell your grandchildren."

"Gee." Abby glared as she rose to her feet, then tossed her styrofoam cup into the wastebasket. "I never realized the possibilities. If you really think the prospects are that good, why not have us put on the stock exchange and sell shares?" She turned on her heel and stalked from the room, the sound of Laura's laughter following her.

True to his word, Clint didn't get to the office until after lunch. Abby awaited his arrival with a sense of trepidation that she could not talk herself out of. She'd tried on numerous occasions to analyze her feelings for him, but to no avail. She was, she readily admitted, attracted to him. And, thanks to his rather unorthodox behavior, had gotten over a portion of her initial resentment of him. But she still wasn't ready to admit to the peculiar sensation that coursed through her veins each time he entered a room, or acknowledge that the reason for the unsteadiness of her hands when he approached her desk was the surge of electricity that permeated the air when he came near. Nor was she ready to confess to the strange sense of satisfaction she enjoyed when they became involved in one of their clashes.

Now those clashes had taken on an entirely different tone. A more personal element had been added. Was she capable of acting as though

95

nothing had happened between them? she wondered, then became annoyed with herself for doubting her ability to do so. *Exert some of this newfound independence you're so proud of,* she told herself sternly. *I seriously doubt your esteemed boss is overly concerned about a couple of kisses—and neither should you be.*

With a resigned shake of her head she resumed work on the file she had been busy with before her coffee break. There seemed to be an endless number of memos and structural reports to be added for Clint to go over. It also appeared as if everyone remotely connected with the company had decided to call that morning, and within thirty minutes Abby had a stack of messages for her boss and had made several appointments as well. When the phone sounded again the moment she replaced the receiver, she was tempted to yank it out and hurl it across the room.

"This is Mrs. Dunbar. May I help you?" she said pleasantly instead.

"You certainly can," Julian Larson said with a chuckle. "How would you like to make your first jump tomorrow?"

"Tomorrow?" Abby squeaked, all the brave words she'd spoken and the confidence she'd felt regarding this crazy desire to float through the air fading now that she was faced with a definite countdown.

"You're not getting cold feet, are you?" Julian teased in his deep voice.

"Of course not," she replied quickly. "What time tomorrow?" she asked, hoping she would suddenly remember some heretofore forgotten appointment and have to cancel this date, which she was momentarily certain would end up in disaster.

"We'll need to be at the airport in the morning at nine o'clock sharp. You will get a full four to five hours of instruction, then make your jump tomorrow afternoon, providing weather conditions are what they should be. They're waiting now to hear from me whether or not you want to be in the class."

"Certainly I want to be in the class," Abby assured him weakly. "But what exactly do you mean about weather conditions? Are we in for some sort of storm?" she asked hopefully.

"Looks like a perfect day for jumping." Julian laughed. "And, Abby, don't be embarrassed if you're scared out of your gourd. It usually is very frightening trying to psych oneself up for such an undertaking. But after you get with others who'll be making the jump with you and realize they are experiencing the same fears, it won't be so bad."

"Oh, Julian, I hope so," she exclaimed on the rush of a nervous breath just as the door opened and Clint walked in. Abby met the questioning gray of his eyes across the room, feeling like a child caught with her hand in the cookie jar.

"I promise," Julian said, trying to boost her sagging confidence. "Besides, I'll be there," he added cockily. "What could possibly happen to you with me looking after you?"

"Nothing, I suppose." Abby laughed nervously.

"That's the spirit. I'll pick you up at eight thirty in the morning. Okay?"

"Eight thirty in the morning," she muttered without a great deal of enthusiasm. "I'll be ready." She replaced the receiver.

Clint, who had walked over and was now sitting on one corner of her desk and making no effort to hide the fact that he was listening to her conversation, dropped a fat manila folder in front of her. "There are several pages of specifications and some additional quotes in there that need to be copied and sent to the various department heads." Instead of getting up and going on into his office, he continued to stare at Abby. "Are you going somewhere for the weekend with this *Julian* character?"

"Not for the weekend," she answered, her thoughts still in a whirl from the phone conversation. "He's picking me up in the morning and taking me to the airport."

"Oh? Then you're going away for the weekend alone?" Clint continued to press her.

Annoyed by this persistent questioning and more than a little rattled by what tomorrow held, Abby glared at him. "I'm not going anywhere for the weekend," she said stingingly. "I'm simply going to make my first jump tomorrow, and Julian is going with me."

"What the hell do you mean, jump?" Clint asked sharply, his dark brows becoming a straight line above the bridge of his prominent nose.

"Skydiving, free falling—whatever you want to

call it. I'll make my jump tomorrow afternoon, after several hours of instruction."

"The hell you will," Clint yelled like a wounded bear. He braced his fists on the desk, then leaned uncomfortably close to her. "You've got no business flinging yourself out of airplanes, for Pete's sake!"

"Just to prove that one can be polite even when forced to deal with an individual who strives to be the consummate ass, I will begin by informing you that every safety precaution is taken. I'll spend hours listening and being shown how to fall, land, and roll." She eyed him narrowly. "Your concern is touching, but hardly necessary."

Clint bounded to his feet, the depth of his anger striking her like some visible force. "We'll discuss this at dinner this evening," he said bitingly, then turned on his heel and headed for the door of his office.

"If that's the case, then I suggest we cancel our date," Abby hurled at him. "I will jump tomorrow, and nothing you or anyone else can say or do will stop me."

Clint stood in the doorway, his face taut with anger, the knuckles of one hand white as he gripped the knob. "I don't choose to cancel our date, Mrs. Dunbar, and we *will* discuss this senseless desire you have to fly like a damn bird."

"Better a bird than a complete jackass," Abby yelled before he could slam the door shut. She swung back around in her chair, muttering all sorts of evil imprecations against her employer as she stared unseeingly into space.

The tension between Abby and Clint became more pronounced during the course of the afternoon. When quitting time came, she was ready to scream with frustration. She'd been tempted on more than one occasion to march into his office and break their date, but common sense told her it would be a wasted effort. For unless she intended to go into hiding immediately upon leaving the office and not arrive at her apartment until midnight or after, her chances of avoiding him were nil.

Adding to her problems was the fact that Laura's car was in the shop, and she would be riding home with Abby. These arrangements had been made when they'd had lunch together. Now, with Clint having slammed around the office all afternoon like a giant sorehead, and Laura and James having made no effort to mask their curiosity as they watched their boss and his trusty assistant growl and snarl at each other, Abby knew she would be in for a session of Twenty Questions the moment she was alone with her friend.

Laura didn't disappoint her. "What on earth is going on between you and Clint?" she asked as soon as they were in the car. "The office has been like a war zone all afternoon. Did he find out about the Major?"

"The answer to your last question is no. As for the first one, he heard me talking with Julian. I make my first jump tomorrow. Naturally *Mr. Weston*, thinking he's entitled to rule the entire world, was quick to voice his opinion on the matter. He started out by informing me that I would do no such a thing."

"Uh-oh." Laura pursed her lips knowingly. "It's obvious dear Clint isn't in the know regarding other men in your life telling you what to do, is he?"

"No," Abby said shortly, and then relented slightly. "How could he be? We've only known each other for a month. But it wasn't his concern that made me so mad. It was his incredible nerve in unequivocally stating that my jumping was out of the question. And not only have we spent the entire afternoon scrapping about this, but I'd promised to have dinner with him. You can imagine what the evening will be like."

Laura, for once having little to say, stared thoughtfully out the car window as they rode along. She'd honestly never dreamed, when Abby started working for Clint, that he would become so protective of her. Never, Laura thought, had she known him to take a personal interest in an employee. But that certainly wasn't the case with Abby. What had started out as an amusing turn of events now struck Laura as anything but that.

Abby was an innocent when it came to men— especially men in Clint Weston's league. Even her marriage to Corey hadn't been education enough to prepare her for the loaded guns of charm fired so effortlessly by her boss. *No*, Laura decided as she pondered the outcome and saw nothing but a broken heart for Abby, *I'm afraid this is one time when Clint's escapades aren't as funny as they've been in the past.*

Very little was said during the drive home. As Abby turned into the parking lot she gave Laura a brief smile. "Don't look so forlorn. From the beginning you thought it would be just the thing for Clint and me to get together. Well, in a manner of speaking, we have gotten together. I realize I'm far from the sophisticated type of woman he normally dates, but even us shy, retiring gals can rise to the occasion when we have to."

"That's the problem," Laura said in one of her rare moments of seriousness. "You shouldn't have to rise to the occasion. When I urged you to interview for the job with Clint, I thought it would be just that, a job."

"Isn't it?" Abby softly asked, seeing the concern on her friend's face and touched by it.

"Yes and no. You've shaken off the Major's influence, and you've become an independent, self-sustaining individual. I'm proud of you. But becoming involved with Clint is hardly what I'd suggest as the finishing touch to your education, honey." Laura frowned. "I'll admit it's been amusing watching the two of you fuss and argue your way through these first few weeks. But this afternoon I saw how possessive Clint had become, and I realized it was no longer funny."

Abby parked the car, then leaned over and patted Laura on the hand. "You worry too much. He's not some sort of bluebeard, about to whisk me away and ravish me against my will. And if it's any comfort to you, I'm just as puzzled by this attraction that's sprung up between us as you are. But I'm not going to stick my head in the sand and pretend it isn't there, nor am I going to run from it. I might even *have* an affair with him—with my eyes wide open and with the full knowledge that it *is* an affair and not a lifelong commitment."

"Good heavens!" Laura spluttered. "You're really serious, aren't you?" Her voice registered shocked dismay.

"Serious that one day I'll probably go to bed with a man? That the odds of my remaining celibate for the rest of my life are slim? That marriage, at the moment, holds no appeal for me?"

"I knew you'd changed," Laura muttered in an unsure voice, "but I never realized until this moment how much."

"You don't approve?" Abby put the question to her gently.

"I—" Her friend of many years shrugged. "I approve—if you know what you're getting into."

"Does anyone ever really know, Laura? I mean, look at me. I've been protected all my life. Protected to the point that I was literally pathetic. I think I need to experience life—the good and the bad—in order to grow, to mature into what I think a well-rounded person is. I certainly can't do that by running away each time I find myself in a situation that's new or uncertain," Abby explained. She glanced down at her watch. "I'm also going to be late for my date if I don't hurry."

"And we mustn't keep Clint baby waiting,

must we?" Laura remarked acidly as she opened the door and stepped out of the car.

Both were silent as they entered the courtyard of the complex, which each apartment over-looked and where the pool was located. Laura's brief smile and her "Have fun" as they went their separate ways brought a wry twist to Abby's attractive mouth.

Talk is cheap, she told herself as she closed the door, then leaned back against it, one corner of her bottom lip caught between her teeth, a pensive expression on her face. *Every word I said to Laura sounded great.* Then she thought back to her attempt to feign cool indifference with Clint. *God! What a fraud! Indifference, according to Webster, is a lack of interest or concern. And that, Abby, my girl, hardly describes your attitude to-ward your boss, does it? If you were any more interested, you would resemble a flaming light-house,* she thought remorsefully.

She pushed away from the door and slowly walked toward the kitchen, dropping her purse onto the sofa as she passed it. One thing she'd learned from her life with her father was how to mix an excellent drink. Usually she didn't depend on alcohol, but, then, *usually* she wasn't subjected to someone as intimidating as Clint Weston, especially when he was trying to impress her with the arguments against skydiving.

The occasion definitely called for a no-frills sort of drink, something like bourbon and water or perhaps scotch. The choice really wasn't of great importance. It was a feeble quest for the courage she would need to face what lay ahead tomorrow, plus, she hoped, a greater command of the situation she would find herself in this evening. After making her drink, she took a sip, grimaced, and then carried it with her to the bedroom.

Some thirty minutes later she stepped out of the bathroom, a large towel snugly wrapped around her small body. One hand held the ends of the towel between her breasts, the other clutched the almost empty glass. With the generous portion of scotch warming her veins and adding a certain cockiness to her walk, she felt ready to go bear hunting with a switch. Even if the bear did happen to be Clint Weston.

"Will there be anything else, sir?" the soft-spoken waiter asked as he looked from Clint to Abby. "Perhaps another drink for the young lady?"

Abby placed her forearms on the edge of the table and leaned forward, her head tilted engagingly as she smiled at the attractive young man. "Another drink sounds perfect." Without even looking at him she could feel Clint's disapproval.

From the moment he'd picked her up at her apartment, the cold war declared earlier in the afternoon at the office had continued. All through dinner Abby had managed to ignore his boorish manners, smiling and talking as though they were on the friendliest of terms. Skydiving hadn't been mentioned, but she had a pretty good idea the subject was about to be broached.

"Need I point out that you are going to have one hell of a hangover in the morning?" Clint admonished her disapprovingly the moment they were alone. "And do you find it absolutely necessary to flirt with that blond-headed Adonis?"

"Nonsense, this is only my third, and you're right"—she grinned impishly—"he is rather cute, isn't he?"

"Cute, hell," Clint sneered. "Yeah—I suppose he's cute if you go for the sort of man that spends hours in front of a mirror." He leaned back in his chair, his gaze narrowed as he watched Abby. "What about your friend Julian? Does he carry a can of spray net in his back pocket?"

Before Abby could answer, her drink materialized. She smiled at "Adonis," the smile turning into a chuckle as she thought of the mammoth-sized Julian and his full, shaggy beard. "He's *different,* but nice."

"Naturally," Clint said icily. "But, then, so are Major Ransom and Cal Densen and who knows how many others. By the way, does your aging major know you plan to try to kill yourself tomorrow?"

"Er—no." She pretended confusion. "I don't think I mentioned it. But I'm sure he wouldn't mind. Even though he's a tad bit older than I am, he's very hip—if you get my meaning."

"At the moment I'm not interested in how hip your 'friend' is, damn it," he said angrily. "What I am concerned about is this crazy notion you have of making that ridiculous jump tomorrow. Has it ever occurred to you that you could be seriously injured?"

"Well, of course it's occurred to me," Abby quietly assured him. "But might I remind you that getting into a car and driving on today's highways involves a far greater risk?"

For several long, uncomfortable moments Clint merely stared at her. He knew jumping from a plane wasn't as bad as he was making it out to be. He'd done it himself and enjoyed it. But it wasn't for Abby. Knowing that she would be thirty thousand feet in the sky, dependent on instructions from strangers and nothing but a parachute to save her life, filled him with a fear he'd never known. *But why?* he kept asking himself. *Why have you allowed yourself to become so possessed by this tiny slip of a woman?*

The answer, when it began snaking its way through the corridors of his mind, wasn't one he welcomed. He didn't have time for love in his life; or to be more honest, he didn't want to be bothered with it. Love entailed a certain responsibility, a certain commitment. Hadn't he been told on more than one occasion that he wasn't capable of making a real commitment?

He stared hard at Abby as she raised the glass to her mouth, then watched, fascinated, as the tip of her pink tongue ran lightly over the moist softness of her lips. Just sitting across the table and watching her made him ache with desire, made him want to take her in his arms. He wanted to kiss her until she was breathless, then slowly undress her and make love to her all night long. He wanted to keep her away from everyone she knew, especially the list of men in her life that had a strange way of growing from day to day.

"May I please have another drink?" the fair object of his attention requested, interrupting the disturbing thoughts darting through his mind.

"You may have as many as you wish," Clint told her, "but at my apartment. We're leaving." He signaled the waiter and scowled while the young man was presenting him with the check, his eyes fixed on Abby.

"I don't recall your asking me if I wanted to go to your apartment," she reminded Clint as soon as they were in the car and he was easing into the line of traffic.

"How observant," he drawled. "I've been by your place twice. It's only fair that I invite you to mine. Don't you agree?"

Abby turned her head and threw him a cautious glance. "It all depends on how you act."

"Oh? Exactly what are you getting at?"

"If you intend to resume your arguments against skydiving, then I can tell you now that I'm not looking forward to joining you."

"But if I want to show you my etchings?" Clint asked, unable to keep a grin from touching his lips. "What would you say to that?"

"Well, now"—Abby smiled as she allowed her head to relax against the seat and closed her eyes —"that would be telling, wouldn't it, Mr. Weston?"

"I suppose it would, Mrs. Dunbar, I suppose it would." He chuckled.

Clint's apartment was the epitome of the abode of a man who lives alone and cares little for the decor, Abby thought rather critically as she stood slowly taking in the room. It was done tastefully enough, but to her it looked as though an interior decorator had chosen the furniture and accessories with a total disregard for the client's personality.

"Am I to infer from that rather sour expression on your face that my humble home doesn't meet with your approval?" Clint asked close to her ear, his hands fitting themselves to the gentle curves of her hips and pulling her back against him.

She turned in his arms, the heat of his body drawing her like an overpowering magnet. The drinks she'd had at dinner, combined with some unfathomable desire to tempt fate, lent a mysterious little smile to her face and gave her courage.

Her fingers found their way to the deep cleft in his chin and lightly caressed the attractive indentation. "It wouldn't suit me," she murmured teasingly, "but then, to each his own."

I wonder what it would be like to have him make love to me? she was thinking as her fingers inched upward to thread themselves in and out of the crisp dark hair at the nape of his neck.

CHAPTER SEVEN

I wonder what would happen if I made love to her tonight? Clint asked himself as his arms instinctively cradled her lissome softness closer and he felt the firm tips of Abby's breasts brush against his chest. He wanted her with a desire that was staggering. Even more puzzling was the fact that she wasn't anything at all like the women he usually associated with. The females of his acquaintance tended to fall into two distinct categories; they were either sophisticated, with a hedonistic view toward life, or else sexy and kittenish, catering to his every whim more with an eye on his bank balance than out of any real affection for him as a man.

Abby was different. In spite of having been married, she seemed to be such an innocent. Clint wanted to protect her, wanted to surround her with a No Trespassing sign ten feet tall.

It was the gentle tug of her hands on the back of his head that broke the incredible spell she'd so effortlessly cast over him. Clint gave a slight shake of his head, as though trying to clear his thoughts, then stared down at the luminous blue eyes silently regarding him. There was a quiet invitation revealed there, the cause of which Clint wasn't certain. But whether it was due to the drinks at dinner or an unbidden surge of passion on her part, he wasn't about to disregard it. He was also fairly certain that if he could get her into his bed, the *last* thing she would have on her mind in the morning would be jumping out of a plane.

With a smothered groan of frustration and desire he let his mouth capture Abby's. His hands ran feverishly over her shoulders and back, finally settling on the swell of her buttocks. His large hands cupped, then softly kneaded the taut skin as he pressed her tight against the throbbing heat of his thighs.

The feel of expert hands and the warmth of skin and muscle pressed against her own body left her floundering amid a flood of passionate discovery. What had started out as a game for her was now a blazing, flaming urgency. She was afraid of the complications that would arise if he *did* make love to her, but she was *more* afraid of an incredible sense of loss if he didn't.

Sensing her indecision, Clint swung her up into his arms and strode to the bedroom. When he reached the king-size bed, he laid her against the nubby textured blue-and-brown plaid spread, then leaned over her, a hand on either side of her face.

"I want you to stay with me tonight, Abby," he said huskily, the dim light from the hallway enabling her to see the leaping flames of desire flickering in his eyes.

111

"What if I say yes, and later we both regret it?" she asked in an uncertain voice. She wanted him with every fiber of her being, she thought achingly. But the closer the actual moment came, the more apprehensive she became. *What on earth do I possibly hope to gain by going to bed with Clint Weston?* she asked herself in one last burst of sanity. *Why do I even want to do such a thing?* But there was no logical answer to the questions, and Abby knew it.

"I don't plan on either of us regretting it," Clint said reassuringly as he slipped the straps of the blue dress from her shoulders and eased them down over her arms. "I'm convinced you are a sorceress, Abby," he said in a strangely controlled voice. "Ever since I first set eyes on you, I've been dreaming of this moment."

Without thinking of what she was doing, Abby placed a finger against his lips. "Don't talk," she whispered. "I don't want to hear your practiced line of seduction—the words of flattery that are supposed to be so effective in breaking down the defenses of women."

Clint became silent, his hands, which were unbuttoning the tiny buttons of the bodice of her dress, becoming still as her words sank in. There was a frown on his face as he stared down at her. "What *do* you want from me, Abby?" he asked in an emotionless voice.

"I want you to make love to me," she said without hesitation, without looking away.

"And afterward?"

"Afterward we'll continue on as before, unless

112

you would prefer I didn't work for you any longer," she said quietly. What on earth had come over her? She couldn't put her finger on the exact moment when it had occurred to her, but she'd been unconsciously planning this very moment since then. No, she hastily corrected herself, she hadn't been *unconsciously* planning anything. She'd *known* for days that she was going to go to bed with Clint. She had admitted as much to Laura this afternoon.

"I doubt our spending the night together will be so traumatic as to cause us never to want to see each other again," he said mockingly.

Abby refrained from commenting, preferring instead to lose herself in the sweeping tide of emotion his hands were eliciting as they resumed their delicate, featherlike movements of undressing her.

The moment the last wisp of lace was removed from her body, Abby braced herself for the surge of embarrassment she was certain would assail her. Even with Corey it had taken her months before she lost her initial shyness. But with Clint there weren't any of the old inhibitions. She didn't close her eyes or turn her head to one side. She found to her surprise that she wanted—no, she needed—to see the expression in his eyes when he looked at her body; she wanted to see physical desire for *a* woman slowly change to a deep burning desire for *her*.

Clint sat back and stared at the small, firm breasts he'd unveiled, the neat waist that flowed into narrow hips and long, slim thighs. He'd undressed many women in his lifetime, but never had one given him greater pleasure than this one. Small, delicate—nothing overdone. Without thinking he reached out and cupped a breast in each hand, gently squeezing the swelling mounds, his thumbs teasing and flicking the mischievous peaks into a more frenzied state of erection.

He looked up from this dalliance to meet the enigmatical glow in Abby's eyes. Her expression puzzled him. In fact, her actions for the last two days had puzzled him. And the events of this evening had thoroughly baffled him. Never in his wildest dreams had he thought he'd be able to wear down her defenses so quickly. *But have I really won?* he thought warily as he drew one hand upward to caress the curve of her neck and finally to touch her cheek. *Am I the victor here, or is she? Are those sapphire-blue eyes looking at me but really seeing the man to whom she was married?*

Suddenly the thoughts running through his mind made Clint edgy in a way he'd never been before when making love to a woman. He found himself wanting to possess, to absorb this lithe, winsome creature he was holding in his arms. To banish all thoughts from her mind other than thoughts of himself. A determined look came over his face as he set about the task of becoming master in a game he had no intention of losing.

Abby watched impatiently as Clint undressed, her eyes going greedily to each new part of him as it was revealed to her. He was magnificent, she

114

thought simply as she silently appraised him. That dark tan she'd first admired seemed to run without interruption over his entire body, causing her to wonder fleetingly if he actually spent time sunbathing in the nude or if his coloring was a part of his heritage. Her eyes feasted on his wide shoulders and his long, powerful arms and chest, both covered with short dark hair that arrowed downward over a taut midriff, a trim waist, and a flat stomach to become dense and thick again over his hardened thighs.

She felt as though she'd been hypnotized as she saw him move toward her and then felt the bed give as it accepted his greater weight. A gasp of pure unadulterated pleasure hissed past her lips when she felt his hand ease over the quivering muscles of her stomach and clasp the hot moistness of her inner thighs. She wanted him! It no longer mattered that the reason for the uncontrollable desire she felt for this man was a mystery. It no longer mattered that she'd begun the evening with some misguided idea of proving to herself that she could go to bed with a man such as Clint and remain untouched by the experience. All objectivity gone, she was learning that experiments were wonderful and very informative, she told herself as she felt her body shudder under the assault of his mouth and tongue. In fact, she decided in one last partially coherent thought as her fingertips ran feverishly up and down the long length of his back, then settled on the fleshy part of his buttocks, she could quite easily become addicted to this sort of research.

"Touch me, Abby," she heard Clint rasp as he too arched against the feel of her hands on his body. She hastened to do his bidding, searching out the flat nipples hidden in the hair on his chest, teasing and manipulating them into hard pebbles. "Don't stop there," Clint instructed her. "Touch me all over," he murmured against the softness of one breast. "I want to feel your hands on every part of me."

And without the slightest hesitation Abby became a willing student, ready to obey his every command. Her hands flew like quicksilver from one bronzed plane to another, stroking, caressing as they worked their way toward Clint's thighs. When her fingertips would have only gently touched him, Clint caught her hand and held it to him.

At first Abby resisted. Force of any sort usually elicited a fighting response from her. But it was impossible to resent someone whose body was trembling from her touch and who was whispering a string of incredibly sensuous words in her ear in a husky, sexy voice.

With a minimum of effort on his part Abby felt Clint move into place above her, then felt him slip between her thighs. She gasped with unexpected pleasure when she felt him enter her and fill her with a glowing, swirling intensity that momentarily took her breath away.

When she recovered, she found her body responding wildly and with an abandon unknown to her. That strength in him that she had cursed on numerous occasions now proved to be the beautiful and exciting meteorite upon which they were exploring the universe. He guided, and she followed. He gently urged, and she lovingly sought out his lead. On and on—up and up they flew till the fires of their individual passions merged into one climactic, fiery moment that threatened to shatter them. Their voices cried out at almost the exact same moment, their bodies becoming taut with mindless, excruciating ecstasy.

When the maelstrom of passion was over, Abby felt the heaviness of her lids closing out the world. She inched even closer against the warm, perspiration-covered body next to her and slept the sleep of deep contentment.

Clint shifted her slight weight in his arms, reaching up and brushing back the strands of dark hair that were tickling the end of his nose. Physically he was more than satisfied. Abby had been more than a delightful surprise, she was fantastic. But for once the mere physical release he had enjoyed wasn't what occupied him. Instead he was wondering why Abby had suddenly turned on to him.

The minutes slipped into hours as he sought to find an answer. He was a man accustomed to having everything neatly labeled and filed in its place. His profession and the success he enjoyed necessitated such attention to detail. And yet, he wryly confessed, the woman he was holding in his arms had managed to scatter to hell and back all the preconceived ideas he had regarding her.

He gave a face-splitting yawn and settled his

chin against Abby's forehead. His lids became heavy. Sleep slowly stole over him just as the first fingers of dawn crept over the eastern horizon. His last rational thought was about how pleasant an affair with Abby was going to be.

Abby looked with a wary eye at Julian, who was standing next to her as they watched and listened to the instructor. "Do you honestly think I'll be able to do it?" she asked when a ten-minute break was announced.

"Certainly you will." Her large bearded friend chuckled. "You learned to walk, didn't you? You learned to drive a car, didn't you?" At her confirming shrug he went on, "Then simply letting go and allowing your body to *fall* from a plane will be a piece of cake. You'll love it—I promise."

Massaging the muscles of her neck with one hand, Abby frowned at him, albeit without real malice. "That's a pretty safe promise to make to someone making her first jump, you nerd. If I somehow manage to do everything I've been told this morning and don't kill myself, I'll be so happy I won't care what you promised. On the other hand, if I fall like a rock and end a brilliant, exciting life, then who will there be to point an accusing finger at you? Either way, you'll come out smelling like a rose."

"Nothing wrong with hedging your bets." Julian grinned. "By the way, I tried to call you last night to give you a little encouragement, but I didn't get an answer. Is the head you've been nursing this morning the result of a little too much false courage last night?"

"You've noticed?" Abby mumbled sourly, the dull throbbing behind her eyes a charming reminder of the evening—and where she had spent the night.

"How could I not? You've rubbed your temples so often I'm not sure there's any skin left."

The return of the instructor and the resumption of class saved Abby from having to pursue the conversation. She closed her mind to Julian's teasing and to Clint's face, which kept flashing through her mind. There would be time enough for the latter after she either floated like a gossamer feather to earth or dropped like a lead balloon.

The remainder of the morning was taken up with a variety of activities, such as learning how to jump forward, backward, and sideways from a platform and how to roll. The parachute was explained, along with wind drift, how to identify the drop zone, the gear each student would be issued prior to jumping, and the altitude from which the beginning students would be making their jumps.

Lunch came and went—and soon Abby found herself in a jump suit and sturdy boots, with a helmet in her hands. "What happens if a person freezes and can't do it?" she asked nervously as she stood beside Julian, grateful for his heavy arm resting on her shoulders.

"Simple," he replied with a straight face. "The

instructor places his foot on your behind and increases your courage tenfold."

Abby turned and looked up at him, her blue eyes bright with annoyance. "Will you please be serious?" she demanded in a tight voice. "I'm about to jump from that plane, damn it"—she pointed at the 182 Cessna behind him—"and I don't need some clown making jokes. In fact . . ." Her voice trailed off, her face going very pale. "Oh, Lord, Julian, I'm not sure I can do it." She shook her head, clutching the helmet for dear life.

"Perhaps an addition to your cheering section will help you."

"What's that supposed to mean?"

"Isn't that your friend Laura walking through the hangar door now?" He nodded toward the large opening.

Abby swung around, her gaze zeroing in on not her friend but Clint, striding alongside Laura and looking mad as hell! "Oh, dear," she said quietly but with meaning.

"Is there a problem?" Julian asked, his concerned look darting from the couple approaching them to Abby.

"Not really," she somehow managed to say in an even voice. "It looks as though my boss has also decided to come along and watch." Privately she was seething! What the hell was Clint doing here? This was *her* time—*her* day, and she didn't want to share it with anyone. *What about Julian?* her mind prodded. *Julian's different,* Abby silently argued. It was because of him that she was making this jump. But he was also a friend. Clint was . . . She wasn't sure what Clint was. But she did know that what had happened last night had nothing at all to do with her life today. Last night a man had made love to her—and she had enjoyed it. Today was another new beginning. She was about to make her first attempt at skydiving —and, she grimly reasoned, if she survived, she might find she enjoyed it as well. Who knew? Tomorrow she might climb a mountain.

"Hello, Laura. Clint." Abby stepped forward and smiled before either of the new arrivals could speak. "This is something of a surprise."

"Oh, I just bet it is." Laura grinned cheekily. She spoke to Julian, then turned back to watch the visual darts flying between her friend and Clint.

"Hello, Abby." Clint's voice sounded as controlled as a tightly coiled spring. His gray eyes swept over her small body swathed in the bulky jump suit, his expression grim.

"Clint," she returned, her mouth set in a pleasant smile. Before she could introduce him to Julian or make any other innocent remark, she found herself being grasped by the elbow and moved to a spot some distance away from the others. She raised startled eyes and encountered such a blazing look in return, she rather hurriedly dropped her gaze. "Does this show of masculine strength mean that you wish to discuss something with me?" she asked, determined not to let him get the upper hand.

"You're damned right I do," he grated in a furious voice. "First of all, I want to know why you chose to sneak out of my place in the middle of the night? Were you ashamed that we made love and that you enjoyed it?" he demanded defensively.

Suddenly Abby found herself wanting to laugh. This huge, angry man standing before her was suffering from a simple case of feeling rejected. It had to be a first for him. For several seconds she stared at him. "Contrary to what you're obviously thinking, Clint," she said softly, "I'm not ashamed of anything we did last night. As for sneaking out of your apartment, I had already promised Julian to be ready by eight thirty this morning. Now, is there something else on your mind?"

"You know there is," he said curtly, his features taut with disapproval. "I thought perhaps after what happened between us last night you wouldn't be so gung ho to carry out this insane idea."

"Oh?" Abby asked deliberately, her chin lifting a fraction of an inch and her shoulders going back even straighter. "Was there some extraordinary significance connected with our going to bed together that I missed?" she asked tightly.

"Well, I sure as hell thought there was," Clint retorted challengingly. "I don't think either of us wasted any time pretending last night. When two people discover something as exciting and wonderful as we did, it becomes more than just sex."

"I agree," Abby admitted without hesitation. "But two people shouldn't allow one pleasant night together to be blown out of proportion," she calmly explained and was almost positive Clint was going to have a stroke, so incensed was he at her seemingly casual indifference to what he was touting as the greatest thing since the Wright Brothers and aviation. "As for my jump, I can't think of a single reason for me not to make it. From what the instructor has told us, it sounds as though it's going to be the most fantastic thing I've ever done."

"What if I were to forbid you to jump?" he asked with the tenacity of a bulldog.

"I'm afraid I'd have to tell you to mind your own business," Abby flung back just as stubbornly. "This is something I *have* to do."

"Is that what making love to me was last night? Something you *had* to do?"

"If that's what you choose to think, I suppose it was. I'm not ready to be hemmed in by the restrictions that come with a steady relationship, Clint," she told him quietly. "If you can't accept me on those terms, then I'm afraid last night will be all we'll have."

"God!" he uttered in a harsh voice. "As trite as it may sound, I'm beginning to understand the word *used*, which comes so readily to a woman's lips the morning after."

"I'm sorry you feel that way," Abby coolly remarked, fighting back the twinges of conscience niggling at her. Now wasn't the time for such thoughts. Besides, she was sure he'd had enough experience with women that the effects of bruising his ego would be short-lived. She was on the point of telling him this when she heard Julian

123

calling her. After turning and giving him a quick thumbs-up sign, she took a couple of steps back from Clint.

"I have to go now. And even though you don't approve, it would be nice if you would stay and watch."

"Why should I be a witness to something that could cost you your life?" he threw at her. Abby shrugged, then turned away. She'd taken only a couple of steps, though, when she felt the heavy weight of Clint's hands on her shoulders. Without a word he swung her around, his gray eyes darkening as they bored into her startled ones. "Abby," he said gruffly, "you mean more to me than just an employee—or a one-night stand—or even a friend." He stared at her, his expression rather bleak. "I'll be watching." Before releasing her he bent and touched his lips to hers in a hard, bruising kiss that warmed her to the tips of her toes. "Take care, princess" echoed in her wake as she turned and hurried toward the group waiting for her.

Abby sat paralyzed in her seat, her eyes glued to the figure seated in the door of the plane who was listening to the words being shouted in his ear by Julian's friend Hank Roe, the jumpmaster. Suddenly the young man drew a huge breath, gave a vigorous nod, and then—dropped from sight. An involuntary "Oh, my God!" escaped from Abby's lips as she realized she was next.

She felt like the last Christian, waiting to be thrust into the hungry mouths of the lions. There would be a few minutes' reprieve—at least she had that. It took approximately two minutes for a jumper to drift to the ground. The plane would then make a circle and line up with the target, and the pilot would check the wind drift. If everything looked satisfactory, then it would be her turn.

What if her chute didn't open? she thought wildly. She didn't even have a will. The only provisions she'd made were for Sarge and Fred. *I should have told Laura she could have my antique writing desk and the dinner ring that belonged to my mother,* she thought frantically. Oh, Lord, there were so many things that should have been done before she attempted this jump. Before it was too late, she would tell Hank that she'd changed her mind.

Hank, however, had other ideas. At that precise moment he looked over at Abby, then pointed with his forefinger to the exact same spot from which she'd watched her classmate depart the plane. Abby shook her head, her hands becoming fetters of steel, gripping the edge of the cushion by each knee till her knuckles were white.

Hank repeated his command, and again Abby shook her head.

She was determined that nothing short of ten sticks of dynamite exploding directly under her seat would dislodge her from where she was sitting. And if she ever got back on the ground again, she was going to beat the flaming hell out of her "friend" Julian for making skydiving appear so interesting!

She saw the rise and fall of Hank's shoulders as he gave a deep sigh of resignation, then watched horrified as he began moving toward her. When he was close enough to be heard, he leaned down and shouted in her ear.

"Julian warned me that you might lose your nerve." He placed his hamlike hands on her upper arms and hoisted her to her feet, as if she weighed no more than five pounds. "He told me all you would need would be a little extra push." After having registered this "reassuring" message, Abby found herself being propelled toward the door of the plane.

"I've changed my mind!" she yelled frantically.

"That's a privilege you aren't allowed," he said easily, as though pushing frightened females out of airplanes was something he did every day. He placed her in the doorway and then pushed on her shoulders and forced her to sit. "You've got exactly thirty seconds," Hank told her with obvious amusement.

Abby threw him a dirty, mean look, searching her mind for some equally vicious remark to hurl at him. "You are despicable."

"So I've been told on more than one occasion." He grinned. He glanced down at his watch, then at Abby. "Fifteen seconds—and you had better make a perfect landing, or I'll have you do it over again."

With a surge of outright horror Abby looked down at the ground. "You're worse than despicable," she threw over her shoulder just as she felt herself being gently but firmly pushed from the

126

plane. "You are a revolting bas—tard." Her last word floated in her wake.

For what seemed like an eternity but in actuality was only a second or two, Abby held her breath and closed her eyes. And though she was unaware of doing so, her hand went unerringly toward the risers and gripped the toggles. Almost immediately she felt the jolt of the chute opening and then the incredible sense of floating through space. The only noise she was aware of was the air rushing past her. She felt she was truly at one with the universe. It was also something she knew she would try again.

CHAPTER EIGHT

As Abby stepped from the shower and reached for a towel, she heard the knock on the patio door. Laura. She sighed. No one but her friend ever came to that entrance. She wrapped the towel around her body and tucked it between her breasts, then headed for the kitchen. Any visiting would have to be done in the bedroom while she dressed. Clint was supposed to pick her up at seven thirty, and she didn't want to keep him waiting.

"What's on your mind?" Abby asked, leading the way to the bedroom.

"Need you ask?" Laura neatly sidestepped an excited Fred.

"No, but for the sake of conversation I thought I would." Abby grinned as she walked across to the bathroom. She left the door open and began to dress.

"I don't know how you did it." Laura shuddered as she relaxed against the pillows on the bed. "I would've had to be pushed."

"I *was* pushed," Abby confessed. "But I'm glad I did it—now. Up in that plane I think I was more frightened than I've ever been in my life."

"I'm not trying to top your story, believe me. But you should have seen Clint's face from the time when you left the plane until he saw your parachute open." She shook her head. "He was pale as a ghost."

"I know," Abby said quietly as she walked back into the room, clad in bra and panties. "I certainly knew beforehand that he was against the idea, but I never dreamed he would be so uptight or that he would come and watch me."

"Neither did I. In fact, I was very rudely awakened by him, and even more rudely told to get my—er—behind out of bed and be ready to go within ten minutes. I've known Clint for years and have always thought he was a sane individual —until lately, that is. For the past month he's been acting like a nut."

"Well, I'm sure it will pass," Abby murmured. She turned to the closet and began pushing dresses aside rather than face Laura's probing eyes. Now wasn't the time to discuss Clint. Her feelings about him were as much a mystery to her as his actions were to Laura.

"Will it? I wonder," Laura mused. "I'm beginning to think my boss has fallen for my best friend."

Abby murmured something noncommittal and continued dressing. After listening to several more minutes of speculation regarding Clint's future happiness, she suggested to Laura that, rather than wonder, she should ask Clint himself. He would be arriving in a few minutes.

Ignoring the insult, Laura got to her feet. "I

129

wonder what hidden qualities you possess that attracts the man? It surely isn't your marvelous personality, because it stinks. Oh, by the way," she threw over her shoulder as she headed for the door, "Cal Densen is in town. He tried to call you last night, but you were out." She stared pointedly at Abby, her brows carefully arched. "In fact, I tried until way past midnight." She smiled lazily. "You know, I've always found something exhilarating about being out at four thirty or five o'clock in the morning. Was it nice this morning?"

For a moment Abby paused, the hand smoothing blush onto her cheeks still. She stared at Laura's reflection in the mirror, her gaze never faltering. "It was very nice out this morning. And in case you're wondering about anything else, let me put your mind at ease. Clint has a very nice apartment—rather masculine, but nice. And though my experience with lovers is limited, on a scale from one to ten, I'd give him an eleven."

Admiration flickered in Laura's eyes as she considered this latest tidbit of information. "You've got courage, I'll give you that. I'm not sure even I could have spent the night with Clint Weston and then jumped from an airplane the next day. What will you do for an encore?"

"That would be telling, wouldn't it?" Abby replied smoothly. "Whatever it is, you can be assured it will be something I want to do, not something I was forced into."

A few minutes later, as she heard the patio door close behind Laura and then Fred's sharp bark as he watched her disappear, Abby turned back to applying her makeup. Did it appear to others as if she were on some kind of ego trip? Worse still, was it *true*? Had those years under her father's domination left her with an emotional hang-up that had her seeking revenge against men in general?

She knew Clint was attracted to her. Even before they'd spent the night together, she'd seen that glow, that gleam of appreciation in his gray eyes often enough to know what it meant—and was woman enough to admit she was proud of it. But was it just her, or did most women possess a certain yearning to affect—even control—a man's emotions? Had other women, like her, at one time or another in their lives felt an overwhelming need to enter into a relationship with a man solely to prove to themselves that they, and not always the man, could be the dominant one?

Perhaps it was a sign of the times that a woman could enjoy an affair as much as her partner and at the same time retain her own individuality, her freedom, and her sense of self-worth—that a woman could look her lover in the eye and inform him that *she* no longer wished to continue the relationship.

Is that what you're doing? her conscience whispered. *Is there really such a lack of involvement on your part where Clint is concerned?*

I'm not so sure about the lack of involvement, Abby silently argued, a determined set to her chin, *but I refuse to become his puppet and allow him to pull the strings to suit his fancy.*

A short while later, clad in a sassy red dress with a tiered skirt and tulip sleeves, she opened her front door to a somber-faced Clint. After observing his expression for several seconds she peeked around the doorframe. "From the look on your face I was afraid you might have witnessed some terrible accident in the corridor," she said with a straight face, her lips twitching mischievously.

Before she could blink an eye, Abby found herself being clasped about the waist and moved aside. Without taking his eyes off her Clint caught the edge of the door with the polished tip of one expensive loafer and slammed it shut. Once he'd performed these two seemingly minor tasks, his hands crept around her waist till they were locked at the small of her back.

"My expression is pleasant compared to what it was while I watched you come bailing out of that plane like a damn kamikaze. It's taken me all day to recover," he remarked in such a self-pitying tone of voice that Abby chuckled. "It's not funny, Mrs. Dunbar," he snapped.

"I beg to differ, Mr. Weston, it is funny. You're funny." She grinned as she slid her arms around his waist, then leaned back against the reassuring solidness of his arms. "I can't believe something as simple as my jumping from an airplane could cause you to spend such a miserable day."

"To be quite honest, neither did I, but I have been, and it's not a very pleasant feeling," Clint told her. He exhaled sharply, his breath, as it fanned her cheeks, smelling slightly of scotch.

132

"What's more, several things have happened recently that I didn't expect—that I don't understand, and that doesn't please me. I've become accustomed to a certain order in my life."

"Oh?" She tipped her head to one side and smiled engagingly. "I don't recall anything coming across my desk in recent weeks that would cause you such displeasure." The conversation had nothing to do with work, and they both knew it. Abby was also aware that she was playing a role totally out of character for her. However, as with every other undertaking she'd become involved in lately, she found herself getting a thrill from seeing just how close she could get to the edge of the invisible precipice she seemed perched on these days without falling over the edge.

"While I enjoy my work, you of all people should know that it hardly occupies every waking hour of my life," he drawled in a maddeningly insinuating voice that brought a profusion of pink to Abby's cheeks. She knew perfectly well what he was referring to.

"There are times in every person's life, regardless of how successful he or she is, when he or she inadvertently stumbles upon something that refuses to fall into a neat category. Perhaps you should reevaluate this sudden upheaval in your life. Could be you might find you really don't want or need it after all." But even as she spoke Abby knew the likelihood of his taking her advice was nonexistent. *And if he were to do such a thing,* that impudent voice within her asked, *what would be your reaction?*

Mastering Clint had, she suddenly realized as she stood in his arms with the now achingly familiar feel of his thighs pressed intimately against hers, somehow taken priority over everything else in her life. Not that there wouldn't be other challenges for her, she reasoned, for the new Abby was adventuresome. She was continually searching, metaphorically speaking, for new mountains to climb. But in the meantime, she thought wickedly, her eyes gleaming like sapphires, it would be a terrible waste not to take advantage of the "experience" she would gain from her association with Clint.

"Don't get too cocky, Mrs. Dunbar. Keep in mind the old adage about the best laid plans of mice and men," she was sternly told. "Not only that, but your advice stinks. You know I'm more than a little interested in you, and walking away is the furthest thing from my mind."

"If you find my cockiness displeasing, Mr. Weston," she returned spiritedly, "then please let it be understood that I find these dark moods you've been indulging in the last two days just as distasteful. It's hardly a compliment for a man to tell a woman he's interested in her if at the same time he looks as though he's suffering from a severe case of indigestion."

"Oh?" Clint said silkily. "I suppose you'd have me stand meekly by while you flit from one ridiculous escapade to another, not to mention the men you have stashed away in reserve. There is one thing that puzzles me, though, concerning the men in your life." He regarded her thoughtfully. "Usually a man or a woman tends to favor a certain type of person when choosing their dates or escorts. But with you it doesn't seem to matter. Young, old, tall or short, you don't seem to cull any of them."

"Well, why on earth should I?" Abby asked innocently, greatly amused by his bad humor. "Unlike you, I have no desire to run my life in an orderly fashion. I possess a very healthy contempt for orderliness. My father is career military, and our home was so regimented, one could barely sneeze without permission."

"Military, hmmmm?" Clint's eyes narrowed. "Could the Major possibly be an old family friend? And Corey? Did you swap your father for a husband with the same rigid standards?"

"No." Abby smiled. "Corey and I were like two children playing hooky from school."

"Unfortunately, Abby, one can't stay a child forever. Sooner or later you have to grow up. This fling of rebellion you're indulging in won't change a thing that happened in your childhood, but if you continue with daring stunts like the one today, you could quite possibly wind up with some very painful experiences."

"That may well be." Abby shrugged. "But the choice is mine, isn't it?"

"Is that what it's all about?" he asked quietly. "Are you involved in some personal vendetta for some crime against you in the past that keeps gnawing at you?"

"Not exactly a vendetta," she replied after a

thoughtful pause. "I am merely determined not to allow my life to be controlled by others."

"I see," Clint said quietly as he continued to regard her with that smoky, enigmatic gaze. "And how do I fit into your plans?" he asked finally. It was a question he'd never asked a woman before, one he'd never cared to know the answer to. But why should he find it so amazing that he had asked it of Abby? Nothing had gone as planned where Abby was concerned, not since the day he'd walked into the reception area and found her sitting and chatting with Laura.

"I'm afraid I can't give you a direct answer, Clint," she said softly. "I hate to sound trite, but I've recently discovered that being a free spirit has its good points. I don't want rules or regulations in my life now—or possibly ever."

"That's one of the reasons some couples find living together more acceptable than marriage," he calmly informed her, then wondered what the hell had caused him to blurt out such a damned stupid thing. And yet, as he silently pondered the wisdom of his remark he wondered if it had been such a stupid thing to say after all. Wasn't he spending a major portion of his time lately with nothing on his mind but his attractive administrative assistant? The flimsiest of excuses was enough to send him in search of her company, much like a callow youth in the throes of that first devastating case of puppy love.

"To each his own." Abby shrugged indifferently. However, the casual mention of two people living together sent a cautious shiver up her spine. It must have been his way of agreeing with her that he considered marriage out of the question. But surely he couldn't have been suggesting that they live together either, especially in view of their working relationship. Then just as quickly a picture of her father's face flashed before her mind's eye, and she all but groaned. Were she even to contemplate such an arrangement, much less implement it, she was certain the Major would croak! He would also recover in time, her tiny voice of mischief chided in her ear.

"As much as I enjoy having you in my arms," Clint said, interrupting her thoughts, "I did make reservations for dinner, and we're not far from being late."

"All I need is my purse from the bedroom." Abby smiled, struggling to overcome the rush of disappointment at how easily he'd given up the fight. The jerk could at least have put up some semblance of an argument, she told herself as she scooped up her small purse and rejoined Clint.

His easy capitulation nagged at Abby all during the drive to the restaurant and even as they began to eat. Perhaps she was being silly, she argued with herself, trying to soothe her injured pride, but she somehow felt insulted. Not only had Clint made no attempt to talk her into marriage—he hadn't even given her the opportunity to say no to moving in with him. Her brow became lightly furrowed, and two tiny distinct lines appeared just above the bridge of her nose as she pondered this galling setback. Last night had been perfect in every way—for her. It was now quite evident that it hadn't been so satisfying for Clint.

"I'm very much aware that, while your food isn't exotic or excitingly different, you did insist on ordering that steak," Clint said, breaking into her unpleasant reverie. "Would you like for me to send it back?"

"The steak is perfect," Abby told him in so stilted a voice, one dark brow arched significantly.

"The potato? The salad? The wine? Tell me which is responsible for that prickly expression you're wearing, and I'll have it replaced immediately." He smiled engagingly, his teeth flashing in his tanned face as he smiled against the soft, flickering light of the fat candle in the center of the table.

"There's nothing wrong with the food or the wine, Clint." She eyed him sternly across the table, then abruptly changed the subject, asking him about one of the construction projects the firm was presently involved in.

Perhaps it would be best to put her thoughts regarding gaining "experience" from her boss on hold, Abby decided. Apparently her honest reply to his question about where he stood in her life had been a tactical error. For up and until that moment she could have sworn she had him in the palm of her hand. At least his actions the evening before and this morning at the airport had given her that impression. And though she certainly lacked experience in the art of seduction, it didn't

138

take a genius to see that he had been interested in her—*had* being the operative word.

Clint neatly summed up the progress of the installation of several huge storage tanks in a few short words, then sat back and smiled at Abby across the table, his gaze inscrutable. "Tell more about your father," he said without warning, the request leaving Abby with a strong urge to grind her teeth in frustration. "Perhaps one evening soon I could take the two of you to dinner."

"I doubt it," she said carefully, wondering all the while just how long it would be before he found out that her "aging lothario" was none other than her father.

"Oh?" Clint asked innocently. "Doesn't he eat like normal men?"

"Of course he does," Abby muttered. "It's just —I mean—" She regarded her dinner companion suspiciously. "Why should meeting my father interest you?"

"Everything connected with you interests me, Abby," she was told in a calm, deliberate voice. "Didn't last night prove anything to you?"

"I thought—" she suddenly began, then broke off, an embarrassing blush stealing over her cheeks.

"Feeling trapped by that fruitful imagination of yours, Abby?" Clint drawled. "Have you carefully gone over what was said and wasn't said and found the results not to your liking?"

"Not in the least," she lied with as brave a face as she could present considering the circumstances. Damn him! He'd baited the trap, and she'd almost knocked herself out falling into it. "What makes you think such a thing?"

"Because in spite of the endless little games of subterfuge you seem determined to play, I'm beginning to fit together some of the pieces of the puzzle surrounding you. Whether or not it's any comfort to you, I could have hired a detective to check into your background or taken the easiest way out and quizzed Laura. But I've done neither. Would you like to know why?"

Abby stared at him, the glow of candlelight softening the bold harshness of his face. "Naturally I'm curious. What woman wouldn't be?" And even though what he'd said might well be part of his well-rehearsed line, it did not sound like the Clint she'd come to know. For as much as she knew him to be a gentle and patient lover, she had also witnessed the incredible drive and steely determination that governed him.

"I'd hoped you would come to trust me enough to be truthful with me, Abby," he surprised her by saying. "I want to get to know the real Abby Dunbar, not some hyped-up version with revenge on her mind."

Abby was taken aback by this surprising revelation, and tiny glints of wariness showed in the crystal sheen of her blue eyes. She'd never been with a man who was interested in her other than for the purpose of bossing her around—who took the time to delve beneath the superficial layer of placidness that had been her trademark for so long. Even Corey, kind though he'd been, hadn't bothered to try to get to know the real Abby.

140

He'd been too busy fighting his own personal battle to do little more than use her as a sounding board.

"What if you find you don't really care for the real me?" she finally asked, breaking the lengthy silence that had stolen over them, isolating them from the muted voices of the other diners. "There are times when ignorance is truly bliss."

"But until I can compare the genuine article with the imitation one, I can't be sure, can I?" His deep voice was gentle and patient as he continued to look at her. "And just to set the record straight, my fainthearted darling, I would like very much for you to move in with me."

And for the second time that evening—no, she hastily corrected herself, the third, fourth, maybe fifth time—she felt the ground slowly but irrevocably slipping from beneath her feet.

CHAPTER NINE

Abby declined Clint's suggestion that they round off the evening by going dancing, and it was still fairly early when they reached her apartment. The drive home had been almost as silent as the one on the way to the restaurant, or so it seemed to Abby.

On her way *to* dinner she had felt highly insulted, believing that Clint didn't think her worth the effort of talking her into living with him. On the way *back* from dinner she was equally disturbed, but for completely different reasons.

The things he'd said about trust, the questions he'd asked about the Major and Corey, and his uncanny ability to see into her mind, knowing she was annoyed with him and why—all these things were now rearing their annoying little heads like a row of weeds in a neatly kept flower garden— for gentleness, sensitivity, and most important, his commitment in asking her to move in with him were the last things in the world she expected of him. And when it came to the question of living with Clint, she wasn't sure she was enamored with the idea of devoting all her time and energy to him; the aggravating ass was already occupying more of her thoughts than she wished he would.

When they reached the apartment, it occurred to Abby that it might be better if she didn't ask him in. On the other hand, she reasoned with a rueful twist of her mouth, if she were to send him away, she was positive she would spend the remainder of the evening alternating between giving in to an irrational certainty that he had gone straight to the waiting arms of another woman and enduring the terrible loneliness his leaving would inflict upon her.

Upon entering the living room Abby dropped her purse on a small table, then turned and looked at Clint, who, without the slightest hesitation, was removing his jacket and tie. "Would you care for a cup of coffee?"

"Sounds great," he replied as he followed her to the kitchen. "Do you have something to make a sandwich with?" he asked with a comical hopefulness in his voice. "I'm still hungry."

"That's impossible." Abby threw him a look of disbelief as she set about fixing the coffee. "You ate enough for three people."

"I'm almost as large as three people." He grinned apologetically. "So, do you have anything, or do I need to scoot out and get something?"

"Believe it or not, I don't survive on berries and nuts." She grinned in spite of herself. "You'll find some ham and all the trimmings in the fridge. The bread is in the bread box."

The grunts of satisfaction that floated over

Clint's shoulder while he buried his head in the interior of her fridge brought a thoughtful expression to Abby's face. It occurred to her that they sounded for all the world like a married couple making their nightly raid on the larder before going to bed. *And that, my bird-brained friend, is one of the most dangerous things you can do,* the voice in her head warned her. *If you start* thinking *about marriage to Clint, then you'll begin to* believe *in marriage to him. Surely you aren't so woolly-headed as to want that, are you?*

"I can't believe it—apple pie," the big lummox who had invaded her kitchen crowed like a triumphant rooster. "Tell me you have ice cream, and your fondest wish will be my command," he said passionately as he turned, the pie balanced precariously on the tips of three fingers.

"After you've stuffed yourself, of course." Abby laughed at the ridiculously funny picture he made, standing in the middle of her kitchen floor, his arms filled with food. It seemed the most normal thing in the world for him to be bumbling around like a bull in a china shop while the two of them tossed harmless insults at each other. Lord! She had to get hold of herself.

"Of course," he returned, transferring his haul to a sizable portion of the counter top. "You don't mind if I ease this right in here, do you?" He smiled engagingly at her.

"Certainly not," Abby replied charmingly. "Never let it be said that I refused a starving man a place to make himself comfortable while he eats everything in my kitchen."

"I'm keeping count, you know."

"Well, I should hope so," she said innocently, knowing perfectly well he wasn't referring to food. "You're making real inroads on a good week's supply of groceries." They had created a comfortable atmosphere, introduced a light-heartedness into their relationship which she was loath to dispel. And yet she knew perfectly well that at any moment Clint could shatter this idyllic moment by returning to the subject of her past or the soul-searching questions he seemed to pose so capably.

"I'll have personnel put something extra in your next pay envelope," he offered without the slightest show of remorse at eating her out of house and home. "In the meantime, you might be interested to know that it's not money or food that I'm mainly concerned with, Abby dear," he remarked as he spread mayonnaise lavishly on a slice of bread.

"Spoken exactly like an uncaring male brute," she said lightly. She slipped the plastic lid onto the can of coffee and returned it to the cupboard, then turned and leaned against the counter and watched the expert preparation of two huge sandwiches.

"I am very caring where you are concerned, and you know it," Clint informed her in a haughty manner. He reached for a paper towel and wiped his fingers, then bent swiftly and landed a huge, noisy kiss on her surprised lips. "I don't like this pensive mood you're in, Mrs. Dunbar, so would you please put a huge smile on those delicious lips? I've never made love to a woman wearing a frown. I'm afraid it would inhibit my performance," he said to her with a straight face.

"Really?" Abby quietly regarded him, imagining the liquid velvet of his touch. "Strange," she continued dryly. "I can't decide if I've been propositioned or told that I resemble one of Cinderella's wicked stepsisters."

Clint braced a hand on either side of her, the expression of desire in his eyes producing in her the same sensation as that of descending too quickly in an elevator. She wanted to move away, to put some distance between herself and the incredible force emanating from him that was holding her in its numbing grip. But wanting to move away and actually being able to do it were two very different things.

"What do you want to hear, Abby?" Clint asked huskily, easing his large body forward till the solid front of him was pressed against her. The warmness radiating from him was rushing into her being like tiny jagged flames licking at her skin.

She ran the tip of her tongue over her lips, her eyes dropping and fastening on the front of his shirt. "I—I—really don't know what you're talking about," she stammered, embarrassed. "I thought it was a funny remark. Obviously you didn't."

"As funny remarks go, I suppose it was average," Clint said softly. "However, that's not the

146

point of this discussion, is it? I believe I was about to tell you that holding you in my arms and making love to you is something I want to continue doing for a long time, quite possibly for the rest of my life." He lifted one hand and let the tips of his fingers brush their way over her cheek, down the side of her neck, and along the fullness of one breast. "The way you're starting to tremble now and the look of passion in your eyes are relaying a very interesting message to me."

"Is it possible you've misinterpreted the message?" she asked in a breathless voice, struggling against the flood of awareness his hands were creating as they caressed and stroked and touched her body through the silky softness of her dress. There was only one jarring note. *She* wanted to be the one in control, the one to have him trembling with desire.

"Have I, Abby?" he whispered as he became aware of her stubbornness and increased the electric friction of his hands. His lips had also become engaged in the game of seduction, their sensuous fullness teasing the pink tip of her ear and leaving a fiery trail along the wildly beating pulse at the side of her throat. "You haven't answered me," he gently prodded in a husky voice. "Do you still think I've misunderstood the message your body is sending out?"

Despite the desire glowing like smoldering coals in their eyes, there was also the distinct need to dominate reflected there. They were two proud, determined people, each bent on becom-

147

ing the victor in a game that could have only one winner.

"No . . ." Abby whispered on a long, shuddering sigh. She raised her arms to his shoulders, her fingers fitting themselves to the back of his head. "On the other hand," she added lazily, "I don't think I'm the only one who's transmitting." The hot hardness of his thighs was now pressed firmly against her, a bold reminder of the joy, the ecstasy she'd experienced the night before. And though she desperately wanted to win this battle, a true campaigner must be intelligent enough to know when to effectively *stage* a retreat. The war would still be there in the morning, and other battles would certainly be in the offing.

Clint, unaccustomed to the position he now found himself in, was busily searching for new and innovative moves in his repertoire of surefire maneuvers, guaranteed to bring the most hostile and/or stubborn female into his arms with the ease with which an angler lands a prize trout. And yet it occurred to him as he doubled his efforts to turn Abby into a willing conquest that whereas always before he had indulged in the game of seduction without the slightest fear of becoming personally involved, it was different this time. Abby had awakened feelings and needs within him that couldn't be dismissed as easily as he had dismissed such things in the past. He found himself wanting to wake up with her in his arms, to watch the first sleepy awareness darken her blue eyes as he stirred the slumbering passion within her small body into a full-blown storm.

148

"Why does it always have to be a fight, Abby?" he asked in a hoarse voice, his lips pressed against her dark hair. "Why don't you give in and admit defeat?"

"Why not ask me to stop breathing?" she murmured in a barely audible voice, her lips leaving a tiny fluttering of kisses along the stern line of his jaw. Her fingers, having been busy with the stubborn buttons of his shirt, sought out the tiny pebble-hard nipples nestled in the wiry hair on his chest.

After enduring the deliberate manipulation of that part of his anatomy for a couple of minutes, so that he was clenching his teeth and his fists like a man caught in the throes of intense agony, a muttered "Damn!" exploded from Clint's lips.

With one quick move he swept Abby into his arms and stormed out of the kitchen, not stopping until he reached the bedroom. Without the slightest wasted effort—this economy of movement, Abby had noticed, always characterized his actions, whether he was working or playing— he began to ease her dress from her shoulders, allowing it to drop in a soft puddle about her feet.

When she would have loosened the remaining buttons of his shirt, Clint stayed her hand with a softly spoken "No. This is my moment, sweetheart, to seduce you." He smiled gently. "I'm selfish—and egotistical enough to want to do everything myself. The next time we make love, I promise, I won't lift a finger." He finished removing her clothes, then eased back a step, his gaze touching on every inch of her body. "My God,

Abby, you are so beautiful. So very, very beautiful," he whispered against her lips as he lifted her and placed her on the bed.

She felt the trembling in his large hands as they palmed the sides of her breasts and then ran down her body to her thighs before he straightened and shrugged off his shirt. The dim glow of light filtering in from the living room enabled Abby to watch each move of his powerful body as he kicked their clothes aside with one foot. She watched him take the one step forward and felt the bed give under his weight. She opened her arms, ready to clasp that hard, warm, muscled body to her own, ready to open her soul, her very being, to the white-hot pleasure he would bring to her.

But it wasn't her arms that he sought at first. Abby gasped in excited surprise when she felt hot lips nibbling at her toes. Then the delicate line of her arches felt the feathery stroke of his tongue. She groaned with unsuppressed pleasure as his mouth quietly and methodically worked its way up to the shadowy softness of her thighs. Each of her senses seemed to have increased its capacity for awareness tenfold, leaving her a squirming, wiggling mass silently screaming for an end to the exquisite torture being imposed upon her body. And yet at the same time she knew there was only one way to assuage the need, to transform the agony of anticipation into the ecstasy of actuality.

When her swollen breasts, their tips hard and sensitive, became the proud victims of the marauding lips running rampant over her body, Abby wasn't sure she could stand any more. She thrust her head back against the pillow, her hips arching, seeking out the waiting release hovering above her. When it didn't come, she reached out in blind haste and grasped Clint by the buttocks and pressed him to her.

"I—want you—now," she murmured in a halting voice.

"And you shall have me, sweetheart," he crooned softly in her ear. His words were followed by his hair-roughened knee slipping between her smooth ones, his arms swallowing her in a bone-crushing grip that threatened her ability to breathe. He reared back his dark head and stared down at her, his lips drawn into a harsh line of momentary self-denial. "I don't know what I'm going to do about you, Abby Dunbar," he rasped in a voice laced with undertones of tenderness and possessiveness. "I honestly don't know." One huge hand snaked upward and tangled itself in the dark velvety cloud of her hair. "You're in my blood, on my mind and constantly in my thoughts. So be warned, if you think we've been engaged in a battle so far, you'd better prepare yourself for a full-scale invasion, for I've no intention of bowing out gracefully."

"A worthy opponent is to be appreciated, but a mouthy lover is a royal pain in the buns and just begging to be replaced," Abby managed to retort in spite of the blood rushing through her veins like a spring flood.

A glittering harshness crept over his features,

his expression turning to one of granite hardness. "You should have learned by now never to make wild statements, sweetheart. I'll never be replaced in your life, and it's time I made you realize that simple fact."

And in that moment Abby knew she'd pulled the bear's tail once too often. He entered her then, swiftly and with a certainty that seemed calculated to push her into a swirling hurricane of passion so intense, she might never escape.

Together they flew. They soared. They became lost in the mindless rapture of millions of multicolored stars exploding all around them. It was a kaleidoscopic world of incredible beauty, a world in which true feelings and emotions refused to be hidden.

When that golden-hued moment of release came, Abby was barely conscious enough to hear Clint's hoarse groan of fulfillment mingled with hers. They drifted downward from plateau to plateau, wrapped in each other's arms.

It could have been mere minutes or hours later when Abby awakened to the world of reality once more, her body still clasped to Clint's. Without opening her eyes she stretched first one leg and then the other, her mouth opening in a jaw-cracking yawn. Her physical condition was one of complete relaxation and contentment, the same as she'd felt the previous morning after having spent the night at his apartment.

For one fleeting moment she found herself wondering just how long it had taken him to perfect that special art of seduction wherein his love-making left his partner with such an incredible sense of well-being. He probably began practicing his "craft" in kindergarten, she thought with a rueful flexing of her lips.

"Starting work on another mountain already, Mrs. Dunbar?" the quiet voice said in her ear.

Abby gave a slight start at the sound, then turned her head and faced the shadowed brilliance of Clint's eyes. "What do you mean?"

"Why, your favorite pastime, of course," he drawled with ease, shifting positions so that instead of being in his arms, she now found herself lying on her back with him on his side looking down at her, his chin braced on his fist. "That of quietly but systematically taking two grains of sand and making a mountain out of them. I've watched you, and I must say, you're very talented at it."

"That's interesting." Abby grinned, refusing to be drawn into defending herself. "I was just thinking how talented you are—but in an entirely different direction."

Clint chuckled. "Am I being complimented, or likened to some sort of lowlife?"

"I don't think I'll tell. You're cocky enough as it is. By the way, have you forgotten that there're two sandwiches waiting in my kitchen, not to mention other assorted items?"

"I've been lying here for the last thirty minutes trying to figure out a way of getting them without disturbing you," he replied hopefully as he swung his feet to the floor. "Shall we continue this conversation in the kitchen?"

"Gee, I don't know," Abby teased, only to find herself being hauled to her feet and a wide, heavy hand giving her a neat slap on the fanny. "Ouch! That hurt, you brute," she yelled at him on her way to the bathroom.

"I doubt it," Clint said unrepentantly from directly behind her.

Abby swung about and eyed him with a frown. "Don't you believe in the rule of ladies first?"

"No." He grinned crookedly. "Not when there's food waiting, and definitely not when the lady is an impudent little cuss like you."

Later, as they sat eating ham sandwiches and drinking hot coffee, Clint somehow turned the conversation back to her father.

"Why don't you call your dad and see if he can have dinner with us tomorrow evening."

"Dad and I rarely disturb each other on weekends," she quickly replied, focusing her attention on the sandwich she was eating and paying minute attention to each ingredient between the two slices of bread. All the while she was staring intently at the food, she was thinking of ways to delay, even avoid, a meeting between the Major and Clint. "We're not as close as some families."

Perhaps she was being silly, she told herself, but she wasn't yet ready for that sort of showdown. Her affair with Clint was just that—an affair—and it wasn't to be confused with any other sort of relationship. To her way of thinking, Clint's meeting her father would give the relationship a kind of permanence; not to mention the fact that she was loath to supply the lengthy explanation her parent would demand.

"In that case, I can only hope he'll pay you a visit at the office in the near future," Clint answered silkily. Abby threw him a sharp glance. "The two of you *do* believe in seeing each other from time to time, don't you?" There was an annoying expression of mockery lurking in the depths of his gray eyes. He knew she was lying, and he was doing nothing to make it easy for her.

"When it's convenient," she said briskly. "The next family gathering we plan, I'll be sure and let you know so you can join us. Will that satisfy you?"

"I can hardly wait."

"Good. Now that that little problem has been taken care of, don't you think it's about time for you to leave? In case you haven't noticed, it is way past midnight."

"How nice to have someone concerned with my health," he retorted in an unruffled tone, a benign smile curving his lips. "However, I prefer to spend the remainder of the night here with you."

"Why?" Abby scowled suspiciously.

"Oh, I'm sure you don't need my help in order to come up with some evil reason."

Abby stared in exasperation, but her mood had little effect on her guest. He merely returned her stare, one dark brow arched, his head held at a commanding angle. "Well?" he asked arrogantly. "Shall we finish off the pot of coffee and enjoy more stimulating conversation, or would you like to straighten up in here and go back to bed?"

"Go to hell!" Abby muttered darkly as she bounded to her feet and began snatching things off the table. It looked as though, without meaning to, she had acquired a house guest for an indefinite stay. The trouble was, she couldn't decide when she'd extended an invitation.

CHAPTER TEN

It was the insistent ringing of the doorbell, combined with intermittent pounding on the front door of her apartment, that caused a tousled-headed, sleepy-eyed Abby to jerk to a sitting position in the middle of the bed. There was also another noise making itself heard. It was the sound of water running and a deep, off-key voice singing what could only be described as an at-the-moment-unrecorded ditty. Had she left the television on all night? Lord! Anyone with a voice like that should be forced to sign an affidavit promising never to utter a note in public.

She stared round-eyed, her groggy mind struggling to cope with such a rude awakening on a supposedly restful Sunday morning. Further attention to the persistence of her caller, however, finally convinced her that only her appearance at the door was likely to put an end to the unholy clamor he or she was creating.

It was when she swung her feet to the floor that the cobwebs cleared from her mind. She was completely naked, and she knew with a certainty that she hadn't left the television on. The "gentleman" with a voice that sounded like the mating call of a drunk toad was Clint, and he was singing in her shower.

Abby wavered between trying to shush her shower Caruso and crawling back into bed and pulling the covers over her head. Unfortunately she convinced herself that either would be a waste of effort. She gave a deep sigh of resignation, then reached for her robe.

The look on her face wasn't exactly the most pleasant in the world when she flung open the door. But what had been an expression of irritation quickly turned to one of incredulity.

"It's about time," the Major informed her in a no-nonsense voice as he brushed by her and on into the living room.

Abby slowly turned and looked after him, her hand still grasping the doorknob. Oh, sweet heaven! This couldn't be happening, she thought frantically. Not the Major and Clint! And not in her apartment on Sunday morning. And definitely not with Clint having spent the night and her with no way of hiding it.

On knees that seemed totally inadequate to support her weight, she quietly closed the door—and groaned when Clint made a noise that closely resembled a yell Abby had once heard in a Tarzan movie as the king of the jungle grabbed a vine and swung across a crocodile-infested river!

"What in the name of heaven is that?" John Ransom turned to his daughter and asked in a hushed voice.

"Er—it sounds—like it could be someone in a shower," she stammered, trying to gather up her

158

courage. Her fists were jammed tight into the pockets of her robe, and she could feel the tips of her fingernails cutting into her palms.

"I suppose it does," the Major muttered. He cocked his head and listened. After a few seconds, seconds that seemed interminable to Abby, he let his hard gaze slide the length of his daughter's robe-clad body, then stop when it reached her own blue gaze. "My only question is, whose shower is he singing in?"

"Well"—Abby spoke very slowly and distinctly, the reason for doing so totally escaping her—"unless you believe in spooks, and I'm quite sure you would never be guilty of anything so human, then it sounds for all the world as if it's coming from my shower, doesn't it?"

The silence that stretched between them seemed fraught with years of tension, years during which Abby had often wondered if the man before her even possessed such a thing as a heart.

"Is that what you really think of me, Abby?" the Major slowly asked, and for the first time she could ever remember, Abby saw—almost—the beginnings of a tender smile. "Is that why there's always been this wall between us? Is it because you think I'm not human?"

For a moment she was tempted to brush aside his remarks and assure him she didn't think anything of the kind. But something stopped her. Although she had long since gotten over her anger at her father's treatment of her and had reached the age when her feelings were no longer hurt by his remarks, something urged her to speak up. A crossroads in her life, so far as her father was concerned, had been reached. If she wasn't honest with him now, he would go on forever thinking of himself as perfect.

"I've—wondered," she began slowly. Telling your father that he was about as friendly and lovable as a tiger with a toothache was definitely not a pleasant thing, she decided as she struggled frantically to choose the right words. "You've never seemed to need anyone, Dad. Not Mother —and certainly not me. You've also been very intimidating. For years I was terrified of you."

"And now?" he asked gruffly, his still handsome face oddly softened.

"And now I'm not." She smiled tenderly. "Cutting the apron strings took me a little longer than most people, but I finally made it."

"Enough so to have a man in your shower when your father comes calling?" His voice was less harsh than before, but still threaded with that authoritative ring.

Old habits die hard, and Abby was kind enough not to want to humiliate him. "I wasn't expecting you this morning, and I suppose I could have rushed into the bathroom and told my guest to be quiet so as not to disturb my father. But considering my age and the fact that this is my place, don't you think that would have been just a bit much?"

A flicker of admiration showed in the Major's eyes as he considered the set of his daughter's small but stubborn chin and the unflinching level of her gaze. "I hope the man is worthy of you, my

160

dear. He's lucky—very lucky. Is there a chance of my meeting him?"

Abby caught her lips between her teeth in a pensive gesture, a look of indecision scampering across her face. "That's going to be somewhat difficult," she told him.

"Oh?" His bushy brows rushed together above his prominent nose. "Would you mind explaining?"

"You've already met him. He's my boss, Clint Weston."

"Ah, yes." The Major actually smiled at the name. "Does he still think I'm some old coot chasing young skirts?"

"I couldn't have put it better myself," Abby said with a shrug.

"Does it really matter what this Clint Weston thinks?"

"I'm not sure," she confessed rather confusedly. The two men who played important roles in her life were here, under the same roof. Her father, who had been a virtual stranger most of her life, was acting completely out of character, and Clint was warbling away in the shower like a drunken parakeet. The two of them together didn't bear thinking about.

"Would you mind terribly going before he comes in here?" she asked finally. "You must have realized by now that he spent the night here. And"—she turned and walked over to stare out the window—"before our affair is over, he probably will do so many more times. I'm not real sure why I'm asking you to go, Dad. It certainly isn't

161

because I'm ashamed of you or any such nonsense as that. Maybe it's because I don't want to see Clint with you for reasons I can't explain at the moment. Maybe I'm afraid you will find him lacking in some way. I honestly don't know."

She heard her father move, then felt his hand on her shoulder. "I never for a moment thought you would be ashamed of me, Abby. And though I won't pretend to understand any of this, I will respect your privacy enough to do as you ask. Why don't you give me a call when your friend leaves. Perhaps we could have dinner together this evening?"

"She damn well won't be having dinner with you this evening or any other evening," Clint's voice thundered from the doorway.

Abby and the Major swung about like two targets in a shooting gallery. Clint was framed in the aperture, a large pink towel hitched about his hips, while rivulets of water made damp spots around his feet. His fists were planted solidly on his hips, and his face was stormy.

"I suggest you say good-bye to Abby, Ransom, then get the hell out of here." His stance was menacing, the set of his body taut and alert as he waited to see if the intruder would take his advice or would need a different sort of persuasion.

"Really, Clint," Abby started. "I don't think you understand."

"That's where you're wrong, Abby. I understand too well," he ground out in a savage voice. "Your older friend here is the one who needs to be taught a few things. The first of which is, he's no longer welcome here. I suggest you get this fact across to him—if he isn't too senile to understand—and send him on his way. The second—"

"Now, just a damn minute," the Major, heretofore quiet, bellowed in a voice loud enough to rouse an entire city block. "I'll leave when I'm damn good and ready, and not because I'm ordered to do so by a damn giant prancing about in nothing but a pink towel. I may be old, young man, but in my day a man didn't go parading around in front of a lady in such a getup."

For one incredible moment Abby didn't know whether to laugh or cry. Clint's face was a study of outright chagrin mixed with absolute fury. Her father looked like the caricature drawing of the typical drill instructor tearing into a raw recruit. Both men were posed for battle, and common sense told her that if something wasn't done, and quickly, they would clash right in front of her very eyes.

Disregarding the egg she felt sure she could feel on her face, she hastily stepped between the two men. "I'm afraid an explanation is due you, Clint," she said grimly. "This"—she turned and gestured toward the Major—"is my father."

"It figures," Clint said icily, glaring first at Abby and then at the Major. "The two of you should be written up in Ripley's *Believe It or Not*. You're probably the most abnormal damn father and daughter to date."

"I resent that remark, Weston." The Major stepped forward and clapped an arm around Abby's shoulders. "My daughter and I understand each other perfectly. Now, if you would kindly go and dress, perhaps you and I could sit down over a pot of coffee and talk. That is"—he looked down at Abby—"if this young lady still wants either of us around."

Her murmured "Of course" trailed behind Abby as she decided she'd had enough of both men and headed for the sanctuary of her bedroom. Once inside, she closed the door and leaned against it, her heart only just beginning to return to its normal pace.

What an impossible mix-up, she thought miserably as she stared into space. Everything had gone wrong. She'd wanted to tell the Major about Clint—when the occasion arose and in her own good time. Clint had blundered in like a raging bull and brought everything to a head, and her father was acting—for the first time in her life— like a father. How did she cope with two new relationships, each one devastating in its own way, being thrust upon her? She felt as though she were being whirled around by some huge, invisible force, swooping and dipping, her feet never touching the ground.

How long she would have stayed in her room Abby wasn't to know. For suddenly the door was opened, and she found herself being thrust forward with a force that sent her headlong toward the bed.

She turned and glared at the intruder. "Do you mind?" she all but yelled. "This does happen to be my bedroom, you know."

Clint entered and closed the door behind him,

his expression faintly harassed. "Would you like for me to take my clothes into the living room and dress in front of your father," he asked in a detached voice, "or has it escaped your attention that I've nothing on but this *lovely* pink towel?"

No, she wanted to shout, *I haven't forgotten. How could I, when only a few hours ago I was being held in those strong arms, with those very capable hands awakening my body to heights of passion I'd never imagined were possible.* "No," she said instead, "I hadn't forgotten. However, with you and the Major greeting each other like two snarling Goliaths, your near nudity has been the least of my worries."

"Well, believe me, Mrs. Dunbar, it hasn't been the least of mine. It's not every day that I face an irate father minus my pants. It's damned uncomfortable, I can tell you," he retorted, scowling.

"In that case, I'll be happy to convey your regrets to my father," Abby replied stonily. She bent and retrieved his shirt, pants, and briefs from beside the bed.

"Regrets?" Clint frowned. "Just why would you be doing that?" he asked stubbornly, not in the least hurry to dress. Damn it all, he fumed, he wasn't about to be dismissed like some insignificant nobody in Abby's life. Before her stuffed shirt of a father had arrived, she'd been a different person. He was almost certain they'd reached a point where she was ready to talk to him instead of keeping everything bottled up inside. Well, the Major could take a hike, Clint silently raged. He damned well wasn't about to leave Abby alone to face her stern-faced parent.

"Surely under the circumstances it would be best," Abby said, trying to reason with him. "I mean . . ." She finally shrugged, at a loss for words.

Clint read the bleak frustration in her blue eyes. Suddenly the anger he'd felt toward her for playing such a trick on him in the first place was replaced by a stronger urge to comfort her. He walked over to her, his hands reaching out and pulling her into his arms. "I'll admit this is a first, sweetheart"—the beginnings of a grin tugged at his lips—"but I think I'm man enough to weather the storm." He began to run his hands over her back and shoulders, letting them dip lower and lower with each stroke to caress the curve of her hips beneath the satiny smoothness of her robe. "Besides, I think I should get to know your father better, don't you?"

"Why?" Abby asked, striving for a belligerence she was far from feeling. His hands were achingly familiar, casting a spell over her that no amount of anger or frustration could compete with.

Clint slipped an arm behind her head, his lips coming temptingly close to hers. "No more questions, Abby. Okay?" he softly murmured, his mouth closing over hers in a kiss that was at first gentle, then slowly grew into an explosive throbbing that was threatening her very life's breath. She melted against him, her body becoming as pliant as a slender reed, bending to the thrust and feel of him.

It was Clint who drew back first, his breath coming in short, painful gasps, his eyes dull with desire. "Damn all interfering fathers who decide to visit before nine A.M. on a Sunday morning," he rasped as he stared down at the dewy-eyed Abby he was holding in his arms. "I hope he doesn't plan on making a habit of this, because I categorically refuse to have my weekends ruined in such a way."

The remainder of the morning passed for Abby in something of a haze. It was, she decided later, like watching a comedy of errors being acted out before her very eyes. As she'd known they would, the Major and Clint alternated from moment to moment between being bosom buddies and being steely-eyed opponents. And yet, as difficult as it was for her to believe, at times she found herself more than a little surprised by her father's reaction to Clint. It appeared as though her strong, overbearing father had found an ally, a man of the same determination and spirit. It was a case of one stubborn jackass meeting and giving his stamp of approval to another, she'd thought grimly as she sat and watched them.

Once she was alone and the door was locked behind her guests, Abby stared dazedly at the confining space of the apartment, feeling the walls beginning to close in on her. *You need to be alone,* her poor, tired brain pointed out. *You need to think, and you need to get out of here.*

"Not a bad idea, Fred," she said to the dog, who was watching his mistress with patient forbearance. "I think a nice long ride would do wonders for us both."

Minutes later found Abby and Fred leaving the apartment, the sound of the telephone ringing shrill in their ears. Abby had no particular goal in mind, and the route she took consisted of a number of large sweeping circles and a few wrong turns onto dead-end streets. The pattern in which she drove went hand in hand with the disordered state of her thoughts.

Her feelings for Clint weighed heavily on her mind as she drove. Wouldn't it be wonderful, she thought, to be able to feed all her emotions into a computer, then sit back and wait while it decided the best course for her to take? It would be so easy and above all else, safe. No disappointments, no heartbreak. *Just a case of computerized love—as cold as a frozen fish and just as meaningless,* her more rational self sneered. *You've fought for your independence, and you've won, but you're still a complete coward in matters of the heart.*

The abrupt change she'd seen in her father also gave her some anxious moments. *Has he really changed?* she asked herself over and over again. *Or is he simply playing a cat-and-mouse game, banking on the hope that I'll fall flat on my face and then allow him to take control of my life again?*

By the time she turned the car back toward the city limits of Houston and her apartment, she still had come to no decision. On the other hand, she knew she'd gained a new perspective on the problems facing her—if only insofar as she had accepted, finally, that her feelings for Clint were more than the daring of a brief fling. As for the Major, she knew it would be a wait-and-see proposition.

The same noise that had been ringing in her ears when she'd left the apartment greeted her the moment she opened the door. Without a moment's hesitation Abby unplugged the phone in the kitchen, then did the same to the one in the bedroom. Any pangs of conscience about not being able to be reached in case of an emergency were brushed aside. She was sure that the Major, if such an occasion did arise, wouldn't hesitate to send a battalion of troops to bring his errant daughter to his side. As for Clint, she thought, her eyes narrowed in quiet speculation, that the gentleman needed several lessons in humility, and there was no reason not to start now.

"Where the hell were you last night?" Clint demanded the next morning the moment she entered her office. He'd been leaning against her desk with his arms crossed over his chest, a dark frown cloaking his features.

Without appearing the least bit alarmed by his nasty mood, she calmly placed her purse in a drawer, then pulled out her chair and sat down. She looked up at him and smiled. "I was out."

"Well, now, I know you were out, Mrs. Dunbar. That fact became fairly obvious after I nearly beat your damn front door down and rang your telephone off the wall. I want to know who you were out with?" he insisted, in what seemed to

Abby to be the only tone of voice he was capable of when angry.

"Then there's another fact that should be obvious, Mr. Weston," she retorted quickly. "Where I go and with whom is none of your business."

"The hell it's not!" He leaned forward, his iron jaw rigid.

"The hell it is!" Abby stared icily at him.

"There are certain rights that go along with our particular relationship," he spat at her. "And one of them happens to be my right to know where you are—if not all the time, then certainly most of the time."

"In a pig's eye!" Abby stormed, her eyes widening at the incredible nerve of this pompous ass. And to think she'd spent an almost sleepless night wondering if maybe, just maybe they might have some kind of future together. "The only rights you have concerning me are the ones I give you."

"Which you did, madam, when we made love. You gave me certain rights over you and a hell of a lot more."

Abby was so incensed she could barely breathe. She pushed back her chair and rose to her feet, her fists resting on the edge of the desk. "Listen to me, you revolting bastard, you—you egotistical swine. Going to bed with you was probably the greatest mistake of my life. But it was *my* decision, not yours. It was also a decision that carried with it nothing more binding than what usually exists between two people simply enjoying a physical relationship. I hardly think I need tell you exactly what you can do with any other ideas you might have concerning that relationship."

They stared at each other like two warring chieftains, the pulsing vibes of their anger rippling like invisible bolts of lightning between them. Clint wasn't actually pawing at the floor in his rage, but Abby was almost positive she could see faint spirals of smoke wafting upward from each ear.

"I attach a great deal of importance to our relationship, Abby," he said in a tone that, by its very quietness, sent a shiver of apprehension through her entire body. "You'd do well to remember that. I can also be totally ruthless when it comes to getting what I want. And just to set the record straight, my dear, I—do—want—you." He enunciated the last sentence slowly and carefully, as though explaining it to a not very bright child.

Before Abby could think of something really mean and nasty to say back to him, he pushed away from the desk and walked to the door of his office. He paused and turned, his enigmatic gaze slipping over her. "I'll be out of the office for the rest of the day. Get the specs from the engineers on that Galveston job and have them ready for me to go over first thing in the morning. And, Abby, I'll see you this evening."

True to his word, Clint was out of the office for the remainder of the day. Abby, having made her way through the two huge stacks on her desk, left the office that afternoon feeling as though she'd been run over by a truck. Her head was throbbing, and her back was aching. In general she felt

171

like the very devil. As she unlocked the door to her apartment she was anticipating a long soak in a hot bath. If and when Clint called, she would plead exhaustion, then go to bed early.

The moment she opened the door, however, her plans took a flying leap through the window. The first inkling she had that something was amiss came when she caught the mouth-watering aroma of smothered onions drifting from the direction of the kitchen. The Major cooking? Abby wondered, her brows raised in disbelief. Her next clue was the absence of Fred, who always met her at the door. Apparently her father, who was fond of the small black dog, was holding her pet's attention by a continual offering of tidbits. Fred was notorious for begging.

Oh, well. She shrugged as she stepped out of her high heels. Being an hour or so behind schedule wouldn't ruin her evening. She walked on through to the kitchen with a smile on her face. "This is a nice surprise, Dad."

"Well, now, I'd hoped our relationship would take on new meaning, Abby, but I can assure you, I don't feel the slightest bit fatherly toward you," Clint remarked as he stepped out of the pantry and faced Abby.

She stared at him as though he'd suddenly sprouted horns. "How did you get in here?" she said, the erratic thump of her heartbeat registering her true feelings at seeing him. Damn! It was a curse for a woman to go all weak-kneed at the sight of a man, she thought bleakly. But she did, and it was becoming increasingly annoying.

"Easy enough. I told your super that I was your cousin and that you were expecting me. He let me in," Clint said patiently, her frilly lace-trimmed apron looking like a two-inch square on the Jolly Green Giant.

She could just imagine how Clint had charmed his way into her apartment, and she silently fumed at his arrogance.

"I'd planned on having a nice hot bath, then going to bed," she politely informed him. "Entertaining guests after a hard day at the office is not a very attractive prospect."

"Indeed it isn't," he threw over his shoulder from where he was stirring something in a bowl. "And if anyone, including the Major, should show up, you can be sure I'll send them on their way." He stepped over to the stove and lifted the lid from a skillet. "Why don't you let me fix you a drink? You could sip it while you relax in the tub."

"Really, Clint," Abby began, "I think you'd better—"

"Does a martini sound tempting?"

"What? Oh—yes, that sounds great. Now, listen, Clint," she tried again, "let's talk—"

"Later," he said firmly, pausing in his chef's duties to drop a kiss on her startled lips. "Mmmm, much more of that and there won't be any dinner." He sighed as he straightened. "Go start your bath, and I'll have your drink waiting for you."

All right, Clint, Abby fumed silently a few minutes later as she did exactly as he'd suggested and

173

began filling the tub. *You've won round one, but even you can't evade the issue indefinitely.*

Muttering to herself, she made short shrift of undressing, then sank beneath the frothy layer of bubbles awaiting her. A deep sigh of pleasure replaced her mutterings as she relaxed with her head resting against the edge of the tub.

Her lids became heavy—heavier—then closed as she gave over to the overall sensation of warmth and comfort that seeped into each and every pore of her body. Even Clint and his irritating presence in her kitchen failed to cast a blight on this tiny spot of heaven she'd found for herself.

"No," she protested in a grouchy voice, one hand brushing at some imaginary thing that dared to invade her own personal paradise. But the something persisted, and it was cold as ice against the softness of her neck. Abby opened one eye and found Clint perched on the edge of the tub, a drink held threateningly in one hand.

She dropped lower beneath the fading layer of suds, her movement causing the water to rush dangerously close to the sides. "Get out," she ordered him in an excellent imitation of the Major's best military voice.

"Sorry." He grinned. "The view is too tempting." Abby tried to shy away from one long finger as it snaked its way through the bubbles to trace tiny, maddening circles around one stiff-peaked nipple. "Remind me to have a larger tub installed when we move into our own place."

CHAPTER ELEVEN

"There isn't going to be any larger tub or any *our* place for you to worry about." She glared at him. At that precise moment she couldn't decide what she was more annoyed about, his barging in on her or the fact that his touching her with one finger could leave her trembling with anticipation.

With what could only be described as a sigh of regret, Clint rose to his feet. He set her drink on the dressing table and then swooped down and kissed the tip of her nose. "You've got five minutes," he said hoarsely, then rushed through the door.

Actually she was out of the tub and clad in pajamas in four minutes, struggling all the while to keep foremost in her mind the fact that she was angry with Clint. He'd accelerated the pace of their affair by inadvertently dragging her father into the fray and was, in general, monopolizing more and more of her time, she decided as she quickly brushed her hair and then turned and reached into the closet for her robe.

Her hand froze in midair. Hanging in her closet were several shirts and two suits that obviously belonged to Clint. She glanced down at the floor and saw the polished tips of his shoes lined up with hers. "Oh, no, you don't," she muttered, her eyes narrowed to steely pinpoints. She jerked her robe off its hanger and almost flew from the room.

"Will you please explain what your clothes are doing in my closet?" she demanded from the doorway of the kitchen.

"I should think it's obvious," Clint said calmly. He was standing with one hand braced on the edge of the counter, the other resting on his hip. "I've moved in with you."

"This *is* my apartment."

"Of course it is, honey."

"Then pack your clothes and get out."

"Sorry—but I can't do that."

"I don't like being pushed, Clint." Her voice suddenly revealed a vulnerability that tore at his heart.

"I'll never push, Abby," he told her. "But neither will I allow you to rationalize our relationship to the point where you decide we're not right for each other. And that's what will happen if I don't stop you."

A quiet look of panic was plainly visible in Abby's dark blue eyes. "I'm not sure I want a strong man, Clint. I'm not sure I even like strong men."

Clint made no effort to go to her, seeming to know that if he did, he might shatter whatever slender thread of communication remained between them. "Why don't you stop thinking of me as a replica of the Major, Abby? How about pre-

176

tending that we've only just met? Over dinner tell me about yourself, and I'll do the same. For once let's concentrate on learning about each other rather than fighting. Does that sound so unreasonable?"

No, it didn't sound unreasonable, Abby ruefully conceded, if one discounted the fact that he had arrived uninvited and had refused to leave. Considering his previous display of bad manners, this latest request was almost comical. She walked on into the room, her gaze locking with his. "Is there anything I can do to help?"

But it hadn't been comical, Abby quietly reflected several days later as she sat at her desk. She was involved in the highly technical process of doodling on a scratch pad, unable to concentrate on the stack of work on her desk, which seemed to be growing by the minute.

Her eyes went to the desk calendar, although she knew by heart the exact number of days it had been since Clint had moved in. Nine days! And in those nine days she'd gotten nine telephone calls and more drop-in visits from the Major than she'd had in years.

Their conversations seldom varied:

"I certainly hope a marriage will come of this arrangement," he said each time he called.

"I don't think I'm cut out for marriage, Dad," Abby would answer.

"I'm getting older, and I would like to have grandchildren," he had told her a couple of times.

"You were a lousy father, so why should I give

you the opportunity to be an even lousier grand-father?" she would counter.

Along with her father's interest in her affair she had had to tolerate Laura's needling comments. Though she parried them skillfully, the constant harassment was nevertheless beginning to take its toll.

As was her relationship with her new "roomy." Unless she was misreading him completely, she thought with a sigh, he showed definite signs of being with her forever.

A soft smile pulled at her lips as she thought back over the last nine days and the few times she'd been out of pocket and Clint hadn't known where to reach her.

"Haven't you ever heard of using the tele-phone or leaving a note?" he'd yelled in that booming voice that Abby was sure could be heard twelve blocks away. He'd been standing in the middle of the living room, and his hair looked as if he'd been running his fingers through it every five minutes for the last hour. His shirt was opened to the waist, and he was about to step into his shoes.

"Why on earth would I want to call an empty apartment or leave a note on your desk that you wouldn't get until the following morning?" she asked in such a calm voice that it only increased his irritation with her. "Besides, you weren't sup-posed to be back in town until around nine."

"I cut it short." He scowled darkly. He came over to her then and took the bag of groceries from her and carried them to the kitchen. "From now on you'll have to go with me."

"There are times when I can't be in two places at once," Abby pointed out, reminding him of several projects he'd given her that had specific deadlines. "Isn't it possible for James or one of the engineers to go with you when I'm tied up?"

"Of course they could go with me," Clint continued, wearing his annoyance like a badge. "But it so happens I don't want James or one of the engineers going with me when I can have you. Besides, I never get the slightest urge to grab them and kiss them till their knees begin to tremble. I also never find myself staring at them and seeing them without clothes, the way I do you. And most of all, I most certainly never get the tiniest desire to make love to them. Now, Miss Fix-it, does that answer your question satisfactorily?"

"The heavy veil of confusion has been lifted from my lowly face, kind master," she teased. "Now that you've revealed you are a sex maniac, I'm sure you'll feel better."

He made a swooping lunge for her then and held her high in his arms. Her refusal to fight with him had dispelled his anger. In its stead was a passion that sent ripples of desire flooding throughout her body. The groceries were forgotten as was dinner, their need for each other far more elemental than their appetites for food.

That evening was spent, as were most of their evenings, in an atmosphere so supercharged with passion and need and desire for each other, she always felt as though they were the only two people on earth. And when the morning came and they were forced to return to the normal world, she sometimes found she resented the intrusion.

"But the happy home life doesn't extend to the office," Abby muttered, the words slipping past her lips in a whisper. Her face burned as she remembered the two different occasions the day before on which Clint had stormed into her office, his face a mask of fury because he had heard her laughing and talking with men from other departments. Even James, who had been his secretary for a number of years, wasn't safe from an evil glare if he got too close to Abby.

"I'm beginning to see at first hand what I've always heard about relationships between a boss and an employee," she told Laura later at lunch. "Clint's like a changed man when he sees another man around me."

"Haven't you ever seen a case of plain old jealousy?" Laura chuckled as she broke off a crusty piece of French bread and bit into it.

"No." Abby shook her head. "I honestly can't say I have. It wasn't that way with Corey. And from what Clint told me about his former marriages, it doesn't appear that he suffered from jealousy with respect to either of his wives. I don't know whether to feel complimented or insulted."

"I seriously doubt he's trying to send you a message," her friend remarked dryly. "But I do think he's unsure of you, so he feels threatened by every man who comes into contact with you."

"That's ridiculous," Abby protested.

"Why is it ridiculous?" Laura asked.

"Be—because I—I don't want to be with another man," Abby admitted for the first time. "Nothing on earth could have made me let him stay at my apartment if I hadn't wanted him to do so."

"Ahhh." Laura slowly nodded her blond head. "I think you've begun to see the light at the end of the tunnel."

"That presents another problem." Abby chewed at one corner of her lip, obviously bothered by her thoughts.

"Can I help?"

"I doubt anyone can help when I tell Clint he has to move out and that I'm resigning," she remarked in a voice that was far braver than she was feeling.

Rather than protesting, Laura merely tipped her head to one side, her expression thoughtful. "Sounds logical enough, except where Clint is concerned, logic doesn't always apply. Do you plan to tell him this evening?"

Abby shook her head. "I'll have to—before I lose my nerve."

"You want me to do *what?*" Clint didn't disappoint her with his initial outrage.

"I said I would like for you to move back to your apartment," Abby said, standing her ground. She was holding her hands behind her, and her fingernails were digging into her palms. He wasn't making it easy at all.

"Who is the man?"

Laura was right, Abby thought as she stared at him. The look on his face made her want to rush over to him and throw her arms around him. She wanted to kiss away that awful look of loneliness that had swooped down and enveloped him. But she held back. *I can't give in now,* she thought miserably.

"There is no man, Clint, other than you, nor do I want any other man but you. I hope you believe that, because it's true."

"Then why this sudden urge to get rid of me?" he asked with narrow-eyed alertness.

"I need space, some time to work things out for myself. With our being constantly together at work and at home, there never seems to be enough time to sit down and think."

"Perhaps that's what I'm trying to keep you from doing, Abby," he said softly. "Perhaps I'm afraid that if you really get to thinking about us, you'll stop seeing me."

"How could I stop seeing you when I love you with all my heart?" she asked without the slightest hesitation. Once the admission was out, she found her heart beating excitedly. She loved Clint! She loved him!

Her confession, however, had the most peculiar effect on the object of her outpourings, she saw with a sinking heart. His face had gone a peculiar shade of gray, and he seemed to be having difficulty breathing.

"If you love me, then why must we live apart?" he finally asked in a somewhat dazed fashion. He reached for her then, his long arms folding her to him like his second skin. "I want to marry you, Abby, and stay with you forever. Trust me, I'll give you all the space you need. I can bring more work home from the office. I'll even promise not to talk for two hours each evening." He pulled back enough to look down at her. "How does that sound?"

"Like the true manipulator you really are." She chuckled. "And"—she tapped him on his nose— "you might just as well save your breath, for I'm not changing my mind. There's something else I haven't told you."

"What is it?" The arms around her tightened dangerously.

"I think it would be best if I resigned from the firm." She held her breath, waiting for the sound of his roar to bounce off the walls.

"Strange," he shocked her by saying, "but I've been thinking that very same thing for some time now."

"You have?" Abby asked, her mouth agape.

"Yes. See"—he suddenly grinned—"when we set our minds to it, we are capable of agreeing." He loosened his hold on her and stepped back, his hands sliding down to clasp her fingers. "Okay," he said quietly. "I can't honestly say I'm overjoyed by your suggestion, but I will move back to my place."

"You will?" Abby asked, again feeling positive her hearing had gone haywire. Was this all? Was he going to give in so easily?

"As for resigning, if you want to work out the

week, you can, but I'll have Laura start looking for a replacement."

"I don't mind working until you find someone," she offered in a strangled voice.

Somehow, she thought a few minutes later as she helped him get his things together, the idea she'd thought so grand had turned rather sour. The moment she'd said she loved him, it was as though a floodgate in her heart had opened, allowing her feelings for him to rush through her body like the very blood that kept her alive. *And now I've told him to leave!* She sighed disgustedly, consigning her noble reasonings to the nether regions of hell.

"Wouldn't you like to stay for dinner?" she asked as she followed Clint out of the bedroom. "I mean, there's all that food we bought. I can't possibly eat it by myself," she added hopefully.

He dropped the suitcase to the floor, then turned and took her in his arms. "I really do need to get back to the office and do some work this evening." He watched her for several seconds, his expression unreadable. After seeming to find whatever it was he was searching for, he gave her a very brief kiss, then left.

Abby stood in the middle of the room and listened. Everything was deadly quiet. Both the cat and the dog were at the vet, and the apartment was silent as a tomb. She gave a quick shake of her head and headed for the kitchen. *Food,* she told herself, *I need food.* But after preparing a quick meal she found her appetite had gone through the door with Clint.

Now what? she wondered, forcing herself to consider the evening stretching ahead. If Clint were here, they'd be arguing over which show on television to watch or which records to play or which movie to go to, or settling it all by falling into each other's arms and making love.

But I wanted to live alone, she reminded herself and frowned. *And now that I'm alone, I don't like it at all. I miss him already. Why did I send him away?*

These questions and many more hammered at her brain all evening, leaving her, at bedtime, looking rather weary.

The next morning she breezed into the office, a forced smile on her face. She paused by Laura's desk. "How about a quick cup of coffee?"

"Sorry"—the receptionist smiled, then turned back to the typewriter—"but I'm snowed under this morning."

"Already? Did you come in early?"

"Oh, no," Laura said without looking up. "Clint called last night and asked me to take care of some correspondence he wanted to get out first thing this morning."

"I see," Abby said quietly. She started to move on, then paused. "By the way, Clint moved back to his place last night. I also told him I was resigning."

"He mentioned something about that." Laura gave her a brief smile. "We'll miss you. By the way, Clint said for me to tell you that he wouldn't be in today."

"That's all?"

" 'Fraid so. Gosh, Abby, I would love to stop and gossip, but I did promise to get this work out. Maybe we can talk at lunch."

"Sure," Abby murmured as she turned and walked toward her own office.

Out of sight, out of mind kept running through her mind as she readied her desk for work. *And why didn't he bother calling me?* she thought waspishly. Before she could change her mind, she snatched a slip of paper from a pad, reached for her pen, and began scribbling furiously. When she was done, she took the note into Clint's office and placed it on his desk.

The remainder of the day passed quietly. Abby knew she had never been more bored or more lonely in her entire life. Even James, when told that she would be leaving, seemed unconcerned.

The next two days dragged along at about the same pace, and Abby found herself chafing against the responsibilities that kept Clint away from her. Once he called her to tell her he was going to be away longer than planned. Other than that, she hadn't heard from him at all.

She wanted him with her—wanted to be close enough to touch him, to rub her fingertips along the bronzed roughness of his skin. In short, she told herself, she was ready for them to throw an extra change of clothes into a bag and go play truant. All she wanted was to be alone with her man.

That evening, after a salad and a glass of tea for dinner, Abby tried to get interested in a book.

But after reading the same page over and over again, she threw it down in disgust. She rose to her feet and began to pace back and forth across the room.

"What is wrong with me?" she asked out loud, causing both her animals to give her rather curious looks. But the answer was a simple one, one that had been weaving its way in and out of her mind for three long days. She wanted to see Clint!

Without stopping to consider the wisdom of such a thing, she grabbed her purse and keys and hurried out of the apartment. Once or twice during the drive from her place to Clint's Abby could feel her nerve beginning to slip away. But each time she took a deep breath and kept on driving. By the time she found herself standing before his door, her heart was beating so loudly she could hear its steady *thump-thump* in her ears.

Her hand reached out for the doorbell—hesitated, started to withdraw, then quickly jabbed the button. Feeling pleased with herself for not having backed down, she pressed the button again. Suddenly the door opened, and Abby found herself staring into the face that had refused to give her any peace for three days and two nights.

"Abby!" Clint exclaimed. He reached out and drew her into the small foyer. "Is something wrong?" he asked anxiously.

"Yes," she said without the slightest hesitation, her eyes drinking their fill of his face. "I miss you," she said simply.

"You mi— I see," Clint said slowly, his gaze

clinging to hers. "And just when did you discover this startling fact?"

"About two minutes after you left my apartment. Since then I've been miserable."

"Leaving was not my idea," he reminded her while pulling her into his arms.

"I take full responsibility," Abby agreed. Without waiting her lips found the edge of his jaw. She closed her eyes against the smell, the taste, and the feel of him, which were seeping into her very being.

"I hope you're that generous when we're married."

"I'm not even thinking about marriage," she murmured amid the fiery kisses she was leaving on his face and neck and was amazed to find that the statement was true. Yet on a subconscious level at least, the idea of marriage to Clint was all that had sustained her through three days of self-imposed torment.

"But I am," he whispered as his mouth found hers and his tongue caressed the parted outline of her lips before claiming the sweetness that awaited him within. "I am." He mouthed the words against her hair, a groan of pleasure bursting from him when he felt the shuddering response that tore at Abby's body. "I want my ring on your finger. I want you in my bed—in my life. I want you—you—all of you," he whispered hoarsely into her ear.

"I am yours, sweetheart," she murmured, her hands running feverishly over the broad thickness of his shoulders and back. She resented the

188

barriers his clothing presented, wanting to be free to feel the warmth of his skin against hers, the commanding thrust of his body against hers as he scaled the mountains with her in his arms. "Make love to me, Clint," she whispered, her blue eyes like glowing sapphires as she looked up at him.

"With pleasure, my darling," he murmured. He lifted her into his arms and strode to the bedroom.

No words passed between them as they stood beside the bed removing their clothes, their fingers clumsy in their haste. When the last flutter of beige lace joined the white cotton briefs, Clint opened his arms. Abby flew into them, a tiny cry of joy coming from her. They fell upon the bed in a bronze and honey-colored heap, their arms and legs in a wild tangle.

When Clint would have pressed his lips to one throbbing nipple, Abby tangled her fingers in his hair and pulled him up and over her. She clasped her arms about him, her hips thrusting invitingly against the solid firmness she was seeking. There was no shyness in her actions. This was the man she wanted to spend the rest of her life with, and there was no room for reservations in their relationship.

Words became unnecessary in this beautifully written symphony, with hands and lips and body language directing their energies into a wild crescendo that flung them, gasping, from one peak to the next. Their minds became numbed with the euphoric mist that surrounded them, carrying them through that final climactic moment when helplessness becomes the norm and reality becomes unrecognizable.

Afterward, when the world had righted itself and their bodies lay sprawled and sated, Abby found her eyes getting heavy. She smothered a huge yawn, which elicited a deep chuckle close by her ear.

"Oh, no, you don't," Clint teased as he sat up, pulling a protesting Abby with him.

"I'm sleepy." She glared at him. "Let me have ten minutes—please," she pleaded.

"No way." The tall monster laughed. He pulled her to her feet and turned her toward the bathroom. "March," he ordered, keeping both hands on her hips in case she decided to revolt.

"You go first," Clint told her after adjusting the water and getting out two large towels. "If we shower together, I'm afraid we'll never have a rational conversation."

"Mmmm. Maybe not." Abby grinned at him as she stepped past him and into the shower. "But think how blissfully ignorant we would be," she yelled over the noise of the water.

When she finished, she found Clint's thigh-length blue velour robe waiting for her. She ran her hands down the sleeves, her heart ready to burst with love. For a day that had begun so dismally, she thought dreamily, it certainly had turned into a Fourth of July celebration, fireworks and all.

By the time Clint finished with his shower, Abby was waiting in the living room with two cups of coffee. He gave her a grateful smile as he sat down beside her on the sofa.

"When I opened that door and saw you, I almost dropped dead," he told her.

"I'm sorry for shocking you, but not for coming." Abby smiled, reaching out and gently massaging the back of his neck. "I went through all sorts of negative emotions about you. Frankly, I never thought I had the nerve to come to you."

"You still haven't," Clint surprised her by saying.

"Well, if I'm hallucinating, I hope it never stops."

"What would you do if I were to say, if you don't marry me, Abby Dunbar, I don't want to see you again?" There was a grim tautness etched in the bold lines of his face, his eyes never wavering as they searched hers.

"I'd say, Mr. Weston, you'd better not count on never seeing me again," she replied without a moment's hesitation. "Not only am I going to marry you, I will expect a diamond so large as to be vulgar—one that even Laura will have trouble accepting."

Clint sat as though carved from stone, his head turned toward her, his hands clasped between his knees. "This is no time for jokes, honey. You've got my whole damn life right there in the palm of your hands. Make sure you know what you're saying. I know what you've been fighting for, and I admire the way you went after what you wanted. But once committed, I'll never let you go."

"Thank goodness." Abby sighed in feigned relief. "For a moment I thought you were telling me to get lost." She shifted positions so that her feet were tucked beneath her and her knees were resting on his thigh. "I love you, Clint Weston, and I want to spend the rest of my life with you."

"And so you shall," Clint whispered against her hair—after he had her in his arms—and after the huge lump in his throat disappeared and the unusual brilliance in his gray eyes began to diminish.